Well of Torment

James Fisher

Cover Art: B.L. Gorewhore

Wrap Design: James Fisher

Internal Formatting: James Fisher

Editing: James Fisher

CONTENTS

The sun sets

The blood delivered

The earth will drown in a crimson river

—Infant Annihilator, "Childchewer"

TRIGGER WARNING

R eader, beware. This book explores Hell and the worst traits of humanity. No character is safe, no act off the table. Torture, dismemberment, sexual assault, and more occur within these pages—some of which involve children. Proceed at your own discretion. It's your therapy bill.

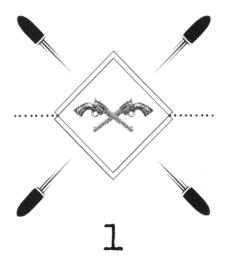

1

RUDE AWAKENING

"Clint McCoy, get your sorry ass out of that barn right fucking now! And bring your Injun pal with you!"

"Hellfire, what now?" Clint grumbled, sitting upright in the hay he'd bedded down in for the night. He ran his fingers through his long, silver-streaked black hair, pulling it from his face and setting his hat on with a grimace.

"Well? Something you wanna tell me, Walks?" he asked, eyeing his native friend in bemusement. Walks In Shadow maintained a stoic countenance, though a mischievous gleam in his eyes betrayed him. Even in the dim light of the barn, he could recognize that look anywhere. He shrugged at Clint, rising to his feet and stringing his bow with a bored expression. Clint spat on the dirt floor, pulling a pair of well-used Colt .45s from holsters on either hip.

"Yeah, I thought as much. Let me do the talkin'. If Farmer Grossman acts squirrelly, you know the drill."

"DID YOU HEAR WHAT I SAID?! GET YOUR PHILANDERIN' ASS OUT OF MY FUCKING BARN NOW!"

The pair walked slowly to the barn doors, where they stopped. Clint cleared his throat, bracing himself for what was undoubtedly to be a foolhardy negotiation. If Walks could keep his prick in his britches for just *one* night, they wouldn't be in their current predicament.

"Mr. Grossman, we're coming out. We're armed, so take this slow and keep calm. Ain't no need for causeless bloodshed."

"You just clear out, and there won't be any trouble!" From his experience, it was a coin-toss over whether Grossman's words were true. Men tended to get irate over people fucking their wives.

"I'm counting to three. On three, we're coming out," Clint said in a loud, calm voice, his thumbs cocking the hammers back on his revolvers. Silence greeted his proclamation. He unbarred the door slowly, bracing himself. Walks In Shadow nocked an arrow, his eyes narrowing to hardened slits. Right or wrong, no man drew down on the Loathsome Two and lived to tell the tale.

"One...two...three," Clint counted, easing the door open with pistols raised. Farmer Grossman stood a good few paces back, a glowing lantern in one meaty fist, a sawed-off shotgun in the other. Frayed tufts of ginger hair jutted at odd angles from his scalp, his pudgy face redder than an apple. A gathering of farmhands stood behind him, all fitted with torches and pitchforks.

"What's the meaning of this commotion?" Clint asked, holstering a gun and pulling a cigarette tin from his breast pocket. He flicked the case open, pulling a smoke free in clenched teeth. After lighting it, he re-drew his offhand gun, smoking and staring the rude congregation down.

"Well?" he asked again, growing impatience peaking through in his tone.

"You've some fucking nerve to be getting indignant with me, *boy*. Don't you lie and act like you ain't consorted with my wife! I found long black hairs in my bed. Wife cooing and flustered like a fucking schoolgirl!" Grossman spat, his voice both tremulous and angry. A tear ran down his pudgy pace–a sign that things were about to get out of hand.

Clint and Walks In Shadow tensed, the big man weeping openly. They both knew not to underestimate a man who cried when he got angry. A man who screamed was apt to throw a punch, but a crying man? A crying man would kill you without so much as a warning. Just as Clint fixed his mouth to de-escalate the situation, the inevitable happened.

Grossman raised his shotgun, aiming dual barrels of hatred in Clint's direction. Time's relativity ceased, the air thicker than a cauldron of stewing innards. Farmhands raised their pointed tools, charging as though suspended in molasses. Clint aimed both barrels at the farmer's head and squeezed the triggers.

.45 bullets whistled through the air, rotating in tight spirals towards their quarry. Each round hatefully tore through cornea, then iris, then lens–plunging through bone and gray matter, leaving a massive pair of exit wounds. Time resumed–Farmer Grossman slumping to his knees in the dirt, then keeling over onto his side. The contents of his excavated cranium spewed onto the soil, forming a grisly puddle of liquified slop.

Clint scowled, staring daggers at the motley crew before him. Much of their vigor had diminished, expressions dumbfounded and mouths agape. He exhaled a large gout of smoke from his nostrils, spitting the burned-down cigarette.

"From where I'm standing, y'all have two choices," Clint said, his steely blue eyes glowing in ferocity. The handful of hicks passing themselves off as a mob stood, silent and hanging onto his every word. With just two bullets, the tide of their intended assault had turned.

"Y'all can report Farmer Grossman's death to your sheriff. He'll tell you himself that I acted rightfully in self defense. Grossman receives a burial, Mrs. Grossman goes into mourning, and you lot go about your lives."

"And what would our other choice be, Doctor Asshole?!" a ballsy hick spat, approving murmurs rippling throughout the men surrounding him.

"Option number two–you get pelted with arrows or shot by my remaining bullets." Clint cocked back both hammers back on his Colts. A few heads turned at his words. Walks In Shadow stood behind them, his bowstring half cocked and brows knit in determination. Clint smirked, knowing damn well the question in all their minds:

How'd he get there so quickly?

He spit, giving the moronic gathering a moment to make their decision. As expected, a few men hauled Grossman's cadaver away, the rest trailing behind with their tails tucked between their legs. They were silent, but for the whispering blades of grass rustling in their wake. Once the last of the mob disappeared into the moonlit night, Clint nodded meaningfully towards the barn, his eyes locked with Walks'. The Native slung his bow, his slender form slinking through the dark. Walks In Shadow returned from the barn a moment later, their horses trailing by leather leads.

The Loathsome Two rode away at a light trot. Clint sat atop his Appaloosa, Walks In Shadow sat astride his Buckskin, both stallions. For a time, Clint focused on the steady, rhythmic clopping of hooves on hard-packed soil. Eventually, the words he'd been choking back since awakening slipped through.

"Walks, why couldn't you just wait two more days? Murrayville has two good brothels, not to mention plenty of women who ain't married. Her pussy could *not* have been worth the hassle."

Walks In Shadow rode silently, considering his words with a small smile plastered upon his dark face. That look was one that never failed to get under Clint's skin–it made him want to knock the fuck's teeth out, if he was being honest. After a few more moments of smug silence, he finally responded.

"Clint, do you know why men still hunt deer, despite the abundance of beef?" Walks In Shadow asked, pulling his long, black hair back and tying it with a small leather loop.

"Hell, I don't know, Walks. It's free, and it tastes better," Clint said gruffly, pulling his tin out and lighting as smoke as they trotted through the darkness.

"That's part of it, yes. And do you know *why* it tastes better?" That annoying grin spread further across his face.

"Please, enlighten me."

"Because you have to work for it. The meat is more tender–sweeter–juicier. *That's* why I *had* to fuck Widow Grossman."

The pair rode in silence for a while. Then, without warning, Clint burst into leathery peels of laughter. Walks In Shadow grinned, small plumes of dust kicking up behind their mounts.

"Boy, you ain't right. But I reckon I wouldn't have it any other way," Clint said between chuckles, his smoke wobbling in the corner of his upturned mouth. "You're lucky he mistook your hair for mine."

"I was counting on it. That's one of the good things about riding with you. It isn't your charm that keeps me around." Another raucous burst of laughter rang out, both men howling in amusement.

They rode through plains, across rolling hills, the night air chilling their skin and whipping their hair back. A moon the color of curdled milk sat over them, the heavens a swirl of bruises. Blues so dark they appeared black melded into reddish purples, sickly green framing their lunar illumination. Cicadas and night birds sang their song, the air rich with the scent of pine. Once they had reached the wilderness near Gillisberg, they halted and made camp.

Clint hitched the horses while Walks gathered twigs and brush for the fire. They went about their tasks silently, the sounds of the night bathing them in tranquility. Clint retrieved flint and steel from a riding bag on his horse, then worked the kindling into a small flame. He fed the fire until a few thick limbs crinkled, the smoke both sweet and acrid.

Walks In Shadow disappeared into the darkness beyond the fire, bow in hand. Clint settled in, pulling out a flask and another smoke. His thoughts flowed freely in the still calm–memories from a hard life. Each drag on his cigarette grounded him in the *now*, each swig of whiskey chipped away at memories that poisoned him like a cancer.

His pale blue eyes stared vacantly forward–into the rolling flames–orange, red, and yellow tongues lapping the wood like ravenous wolves over a severed femur. The fire called to him, pushing him violently into the one memory drink could not touch. A small home ablaze. Hellishly agonized wails cutting over the din of whooping miscreants and roaring flames. Charred remnants–husks–no longer fit to be described as human.

Clint's Stygian vortex of thoughts abruptly halted, crunching brush in the darkness pulling his attention. Walks In Shadow came into view, emerging from darkness with a fat rabbit in tow. His posture relaxed, and he holstered the Colt he'd drawn without a thought. Walks skinned and gutted his kill, running a skewer through its mouth and out its ass. He tended to the rabbit, rotating it every so often. Rendered fat ran rivers down the succulent muscle strands, the meat's aroma rich and enticing.

Clint took another glug of whiskey, lighting a fresh cigarette as he watched the rabbit cook. The two men sat in silence, eyeing their meal gratefully.

"That's a good kill, Walks. Been a while since we've had a rabbit. Damn sure beats that stew Farmer Grossman served us. I took one bite and knew that meat had turned." Clint grimaced at the flavors his recollection summoned. The Indian nodded, diligently rotating the spit.

When the meat finished cooking, they each tore chunks off, stuffing the steaming morsels down without hesitation. Clint savored the taste, juices dripping down his beard. They wasted nothing, leaving no trace of their kill but bones, and chewed up pieces of gristle. Walks let out a soft sigh of contentment, leaning back against a large, smooth stone nestled into the ground.

"So, Murrayville—"

"Yeah, what about it?" Clint grunted, polishing off the remaining liquor in his flask.

"Remind me why we're headed north, when all the good bounty hunting is to the south."

"Oh, Hell! Do I have to read you the telegram again? All that pussy juice leave your brain waterlogged?"

"Funny. No, I haven't forgotten what the telegram said. I just don't understand why we're doing this, when money is way better elsewhere."

"It ain't just about the money, Walks. I owe Sheriff Gallagher. Let's leave it at that." Clint's tone was ice, and he took one last pull from his cigarette before flicking it away.

Walks In Shadow pried no more, either satisfied with his answer or too tired to argue. Clint pulled his hat down over his eyes and laid back. The remaining hours of dwindling night elapsed, a chill breeze tracing delicate fingers across the land as it passed through. Dark blues and purples slowly morphed into pinks and oranges. The sun arrived, bringing with it the symphony of nature singing its praises.

Clint rose to the sounds of his partner cinching the girth on his saddle. He joined him, brushing out his stud's mane and feeding it an apple from a riding pack. It ate the fruit gently, his lips barely grazing Clint's palm. Clint told the horse he was a good boy, patting him and unhitching him. The Loathsome Two mounted up and rode on. Murrayville was about a day and a half's ride away.

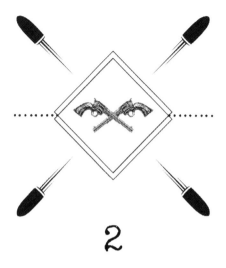

2

TOLL BRIDGE

After a good six hours of riding, they found themselves at an impasse. A roaring river sat before them, the bridge across barred by rough-looking men with mean eyes and rifles in their hands. Clint lit a cigarette, glaring at the ugly obstruction. They were too close to turn back unnoticed, and it was the only bridge for miles around.

"Walks, looks like we're gonna need your skills," Clint said, spitting over his shoulder. The Indian nodded, dismounting his horse and slinking away into the wood line, bow in hand. Clint grabbed the reins on the Buckskin, gently trotting it alongside him toward the bridge. A gruff voice called loudly for him to halt just before reaching the human blockade.

A hideous man stepped forward, caked in dirt from the road with a Winchester slung on his back. His stench burned Clint's nostrils—a nauseating mixture of stale sweat, dried piss, and shit.

"There's a toll to cross this bridge, mister." The bandit flashed a mouthful of broken and yellow teeth. Clint nodded slowly. "How much?"

He felt the man's sickly eyes leering, combing over his possessions, including the horses. A stream of gray slobber ran down his grizzled chin.

"You just give me and the boys everything you've got, and we'll let you pass—" He abruptly halted at the cold iron of a Colt barrel pressed to his forehead. All of his bravado sapped out in an instant, his expression gravely serious.

"Now, before y'all go to gettin' itchy trigger fingers, I want you to stop and think. If you want these horses, shooting's a bad idea. Also—I'll blow this ugly bastard's head clean off!" Clint's booming voice carried over the coursing waters below.

The group of men blocking the bridge's midway point all laughed—an ugly, barking sound that crescendoed into obnoxious brays. Clint rolled his eyes, the whimpering of his hostage simply too much to bear.

He squeezed the trigger.

Cranium and gray matter flew heavenward in a fist-sized glob, blood misting in the breeze.

Time's cruel pendulum lulled.

Tickticktickticktick

Became

Tick...tick...tick...tick...

Clint's eyes glowed, sharpening for the ensuing slaughter. Arrows flew from thin air on the opposite side of the bridge in a vengeful volley. Men's eyes bulged to bursting, falling forward with trembling arrow shafts embedded into their backs. His thumbs cocked both hammers on his irons, muzzles flaring in atomic mushroom clouds. .45 rounds whistled through the still air.

The Loathsome Two's righteous storm of lead and arrows only lasted a few seconds. For them and those who fell, it felt like eons. Time caught up, the raging waters hissing and crashing off the stony banks below with renewed vigor. Clint holstered his guns, lighting a smoke as he surveyed the aftermath with apathetic eyes. Ten men slain, blood and brains coating the wooden slats, giving them a metallic sheen.

Walks In Shadow appeared from thin air, looting bodies before kicking them over the side of the bridge. Clint joined him, and by the time they searched and tossed the corpses, they had a paltry six dollars between them to show for their troubles. Walks mounted his Buckskin, and they crossed the bridge single file. Bodies floated amongst the whitecaps, carried away by angry waters, never to be seen again.

They rode on–verdant and lush greenery overtaking the desert to which they were so accustomed. Each mile closer to Murrayville added to a nameless dread festering in Clint's gut. It was a sensation beyond words or reasoning. Despite the chirping birds and roaming deer, despite orchards of blooming flowers and gorgeous displays of vitality surrounding him, he could only focus on what lay in wait at their journey's conclusion. Although the sun shined brightly on the gunslinger clad in black, he only felt the icy fist of death awaiting him.

Sheriff Roy Gallagher had never been a man to mince words, but the telegram he'd sent for Clint was *especially* cryptic. Clint had read it so many times that he had firmly etched the words into his memory.

NEED AID. MURRAYVILLE IN DANGER. WILL
PAY. COME NOW.

Something in the message's urgency unnerved him. Desperation oozed from those nine words. And fear–a light he'd never seen Roy in before. He only hoped they'd make it in time to help. At their current rate of travel, Clint estimated their arrival at around evening the following day. That was, of course, provided no further complications arose–a gamble, if ever there was one.

As the sun shifted westward and light began to dwindle and wane, they kept an eye out for a spot to camp for the night. The pair found an adequate location near a shallow stream. After watering and feeding their horses, they hitched them.

"Walks, you go ahead and hunt for our supper. I'll get the kindling and handle the fire." The Indian nodded, vanishing into the wild greenery with his bow.

Clint gathered twigs, limbs, and a few fallen branches. He built up the kindling, and by the time Walks returned, a healthy fire roared. Walks cleaned the four squirrels he'd killed and set them on a stone near Clint. He grabbed a cast-iron pot from his riding pack and filled it halfway from the stream. After placing the pot in the fire, he dropped the squirrels into the clear water.

Within an hour, the small rodents had become tender, the water now a fat-tinged broth. They each fixed themselves a cup, steam billowing in the declining temperatures of the night. Clint thanked his partner with a nod, blowing on the meal to cool it before venturing a quick sip. Despite his scalded tongue, he let out an involuntary grunt of approval. The broth warmed him from throat to belly, radiating throughout with comforting tingles. They ate their meals in contented silence.

He lit a cigarette, savoring the rich smoke and gazing at the star-strewn heavens in contemplation. The future was on his mind. No matter what happened in Murrayville, Clint would not return to Mexico. The novelty of riding across harsh sands and gunning robbers and murderers down had died. Something inside him broke in that desolate land.

Walks In Shadow bore the same scars, but neither of them ever spoke on such matters. Although riches lay in that nearly lawless place, so too lay the machinations of vicious demons disguised as men. For some inexplicable reason, however, distance from Mexico didn't bring comfort. Murrayville lay ahead, the desert behind. Clint ignored the dark flow of thoughts, lowering the brim of his hat and closing his eyes. He fell asleep beneath the heavens' celestial glow.

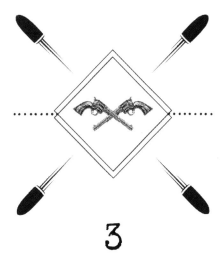

3

VISION OF INFERNO

Hot. It was unbearably hot. Clint held no physical form, his view of the infernal realm like glancing through a window from high above. Billions of anguished wails rang out across the infinite space of unrelenting suffering. The ground was jet black, glowing red cracks that spouted blue flames marring its surface.

Nude men and women hung from cruelly sharp stalagmites, their withered hands extended in a futile gesture for help that would not come. Cracked lips opened and closed, their hoarse cries no louder than the rustling of fallen autumnal leaves–lost in the din, drowned out by fresher suffering.

His vision blurred, zooming across the hellscape. Below him sat a pit, many fathoms deep and packed with writhing bodies. Flesh of every hue glistened in sweat and fluids. Hellhounds raped them, thorned cocks ripping their asses and cunts open hatefully. Intestines swayed with the motions of their relentless pummeling. Shit, blood, urine, and semen stood a foot thick across the bottom of the pit.

The flaming canines of Satan ate their victims after breeding them. Damned souls regenerated, only to be raped and feasted upon again. Eternal anguish beyond all mortal comprehension. Clint's vision blurred again, his viewing directed elsewhere.

Daemons flayed men with vicious talons, forcing them to feast upon their own flesh. Women were fisted violently, their breasts removed with glass shards as they shrieked and writhed. A deluge of sights not meant for the living assaulted Clint's mind. Like the suffering before and all around him, it was cruel and seemingly without end.

Unchristened children from faraway lands were held by their hands and feet. Daemons wrenched their halves apart, organs and blood sizzling on the hot bedrock. Their cries rang out like a sorrowful symphony of alien birds. Clint fought to shut out the images, to no avail. Death, suffering, death, repeat–it was an infinite loop, malevolent and causeless. Blood spouted from the ground, fires roaring across the nightmarish plane. The damned below resembled fleshy ants emerging in panic from a kicked hill. He felt his vision, again, directed elsewhere.

Columns of crystallized blood jutted from the ebony floor of a massive throne room. Daemons in gilded armor stood around the massive space. A throne taller than a mountain lay at the room's center. His eyes scanned it, and horror filled him. It was constructed of bone. Millions of skeletal babies comprised its form–children not christened before their demise.

Lucifer entered the chamber through a gargantuan archway. He wielded a beauty both great and terrible. Blonde hair finer than silk flowed down his chiseled form. Despite his angelic features, evil pulsed from him in an exponential torrent. Shorn wings jutted from Satan's back, cleaved long ago by Gabriel's righteous sword.

The Fallen One spoke in a voice both musical and booming, though Clint could not comprehend his words. His sight faded.

A vision of a town on Earth, set ablaze. The sky was sanguine, the sun now a serpent's eye–twitching and ever watchful. Cries of pain and terror rang out, intermingled with the rude barks of gunfire. A massive well sat directly at the center of the town, belching green and tendrilous forks of lightning from its depths. A town sign, swinging in a strong breeze. It said:

Murrayville.

4

OVERDUE WORDS

C lint bolted awake, his long hair soaked through in perspiration. His vision was blurry, still returning from the veil of sleep. The sky overhead held little light, the sun not yet peeking on the horizon. After a moment, his eyes adjusted, and he noticed Walks In Shadow preparing their horses.

He slowly rose to his feet, stretching with clenched fists nestled against the small of his back. Clint walked over to his stud, taking care to properly cinch his saddle. Once the pair concluded their pre-travel adjustments, they mounted up and rode away into darkness.

After an hour of silent riding, Walks In Shadow spoke.

"I'm assuming we had the same dream."

"Seems that way."

"Hell, fire, daemons—sound about right?"

Clint nodded, his mouth pulled into a tight line beneath his beard. He slid a cigarette from his tin and lit it as they trotted across the dark landscape. Walks released an exasperated sigh and ran his fingers through his hair with his face upturned.

"Things never get easier for us, do they, Clint?"

"Don't seem like they do. Us sharing the same dream–he never mentioned that when–when we changed."

"*Changed?*" Walks In Shadow scoffed, spitting over the side of his horse.

"We never *changed*, Clint. We're still the same cutthroat bastards we've always been. Now, we just do it better. Now, we have powers. But as people? No, we haven't changed an iota."

Clint let the words soak in. They angered him, because deep down, he knew they rang true. Despite this, his pride wouldn't allow him to concede, even if he was wrong.

"Is that really what you think? You're saying we haven't been better at all? It's been months since I cheated at cards or outright gunned a man down without trying to talk things through first."

"Yes, Clint. That's what I think. Sure, you like to *act* like we're different now. But no matter how many times you play nice or try to 'talk things out', the result is the same—dead people and spent bullets. Half-assed negotiations don't cancel out murder, just like gunning down that mob didn't redeem us from torching the house with children inside it."

Rage splashed across the gunslinger like a magmatic burst. His teeth were clenched, his brows knit tightly. Before he could do anything rash, Walks In Shadow continued speaking.

"Clint, there's a reason I'm saying this. If those visions were right, Hell's coming to Earth. Daemons and the weak-minded men who serve them won't play by the rules, so neither can we. Gabriel chose men like us for a reason. We can do things an angel or holy man wouldn't be able to. Sheriff Gallagher can't face something like this by following the rules, so he sent for *us*. The world around us knows what we are. Why don't you?"

Goddamn you, Clint thought miserably. The fury in his belly went cold. There was nothing left to say. Murrayville lay a few hours ahead. The Loathsome Two rode hard, the sun peeking over distant plains.

The air grew drier and hotter the closer they drew to Murrayville. A sickness lay before them, radiating out from its source like a growing tumor. Brown and dying vegetation crunched beneath their horses' hooves, the earth cracked open in spots–dessicated flesh begging the heavens for a rain that may never come. The horses could sense the diseased land. Clint felt his stud's muscles tense the further they pushed through the sinister miasma hanging upon the soil.

Nothing could be done about it. They galloped across the cadaverous earth with tension building in the pits of their stomachs. Clint turned his friend's words over in his mind ceaselessly. Ever since Gabriel bestowed their gifts upon them that night in Mexico, he'd been attempting to bury his true self, little by little.

His partner's short and stand-offish nature held merit, as much as it pained him to admit it. Clint wished he could change, wished the world wasn't such a hateful place. Sadly, wishes weren't worth a hat full of shit. Clint McCoy was a cheat at cards, a drunk, and a killer. All his efforts to construct a more civil facade the past few months felt foolish considering Walks' words.

If Sheriff Roy Gallagher called upon him, it meant he needed the fastest draw in Texas, and that's just what he'd get. Clint steeled himself for whatever lay ahead. Hell was coming to Murrayville, and his trigger fingers itched.

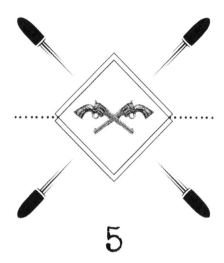

5

LAY OF THE LAND

The Loathsome Two arrived at the far outskirts of Murrayville with the sun hatefully beating down upon them. If the lands before were sickly, they could only describe the ones now surrounding them as long deceased. Gnarled and leafless trees jutted from crumbling soil like diseased phalluses, the black bark and roots losing hold of the earth. Nothing green remained, the skies overhead an angry bleeding mess of oranges and reds.

They crested the last hill, Murrayville unfurling for them below. The town sprawled, a multitude of businesses aligned neatly with the road bisecting it. Large clusters of small houses sat behind the main strip, all simply built and modest in appearance. Clint and Walks slowed their horses to a light trot, descending slowly towards Murrayville proper.

Clint lit a cigarette, noting how much Murrayville grew since he'd last been. They rode past businesses: general stores, clothing shops, a gunsmith, and a farrier. The opposite end of the strip held the brothels and saloons. The church sat nestled at the midway point. Aside from the ravaged lands, he noticed something more ominous: the people.

To someone unattentive, all things appeared routine. Their plastic smiles hid a deep fear, perceptible in their hopeless eyes. They moved mechanically, like clockwork beings advancing, because there simply was no other choice. Whatever transpired before the pair's arrival sapped the townsfolk's morale. Clint grimaced, speeding up his horse's trot and making a beeline for the sheriff's station.

Clint burst into the building without knocking, Walks In Shadow not far behind. It was dim and stifling inside the station. Sheriff Gallagher sat at a circular wooden table, polishing his Colt .44 by the light of an oil lantern. His bushy silver eyebrows shot up comically at their abrupt entrance, his mustache quivering.

"As I live and fucking breathe, it's The Loathsome Two, here at last!" Roy rose to his feet with a weary grin. He shook both their hands and motioned for them to take a seat. They sat while he rummaged through a cabinet in the room's corner, returning with a half-gallon of whiskey and three drinking glasses. The three men each slammed their drinks back. Roy promptly refilled them.

"Clint, Walks–I won't sugarcoat things. Never been my style. Things are completely fucked around here. I hardly know where to begin."

Sheriff Gallagher sank into his chair and swigged back his second round. At that moment, he looked ancient to Clint. Hardly recognizable when contrasted with the vivid memories he still held of Roy. Clint stubbed his smoke and lit another.

No one spoke for a while. The sheriff poured them each a fresh glass when they ran out; the silence laden with dread. Aside from them, the station was empty. The three cells lining either wall held no one, the gates locked shut. Roy resumed speaking.

"I guess this all started about a month ago. I'd find little devils carved from wood placed around the town, or pentagrams painted on the sides of houses. At first, I thought it was just a bored peckerwood fucking with me. That was a bad assumption on my part. Things soured quickly from there.

"A fortnight ago, our first murder occurred. Claire Beaumont fell first. Whoever did the deed left a message near her body, written in blood. When Ethel saw what had been done to her daughter, she keeled over. Lady's heart plum gave out."

Clint and Walks In Shadow eyed Roy impassively, the room again silent. Sheriff Gallagher sipped his whiskey and quietly composed himself.

"What did the message say?" Walks asked.

"One down, five to go. The Well of Torment is nigh." Roy's shoulders sank, a shadow falling across his face.

"If I said Claire's killing was the worst of it, I'd be lying. Not three days later, two more corpses appeared. The things done to them were unholy and inhuman. They were only *children*. Now, the townsfolk are broken and paranoid. I can't say I blame them. The killer or killers left another message by their bodies: four down, two to go. The Well will feast soon."

"*Four?* I ain't no mathematician, but you only mentioned three murders," Clint said. The sheriff shrugged.

"That was my figure, as well. My best guess is that they tacked Ethel's death to their count. I don't know how any of this bullshit works, but I can assure you the threat is real. You've seen the surrounding land. It's all fucking dead."

Clint nodded and finished his glass. Walks In Shadow stared at the dancing flames within the lantern in contemplation. The situation was dire–malevolent machinations with no end in sight. One question remained.

"Well, Roy–you sent for us, and we came. What do you need us to do?"

6

NIGHT ON THE TOWN

Impending apocalypse or not, the drunks in Wrangler's Rest showed little fear. A player piano pinged away over the din of gruff voices and clinking glasses. Clint and Walks In Shadow observed all from their table near the back of the saloon. They nursed whiskeys, attempting to plan with the little they knew.

Nothing stuck so far, and Clint felt an irritation bubbling up within himself. Roy wanted them to sit and wait like a pair of useless dicks. It was a foolhardy order, but the sheriff insisted that further violence could only exacerbate the situation. So they sat. And they waited. And in those stretched-out moments of boredom and a feeling of uselessness, Clint's vice called to him like a long-lost lover.

Grizzled men shouted and cursed amongst themselves around card tables, the clink of coin a siren's call. He stood from his chair, nodded to Walks, and made his way to a table with a free chair. There was no resisting his baser needs. After being waved in by the dealer, Clint sat. The game was blackjack.

For the first few rounds, Clint played normally. He'd be up, then down. The tedium of chance grew too great. He needed to win—yearned for the rush of getting one over on the mouth-breathing cunts surrounding him. As the next game began, he eyed his hand: a seven of clubs and eight of diamonds.

When asked, Clint hit for another card, his heart racing as the thrill of a win grew near. A light glow flickered in his eyes. For those around him, nothing seemed to happen. For Clint, time halted.

While inside the temporal flux, he had ample time to swap the card being handed to him. He replaced the king of clubs with a six of spades, ensuring a perfect count of twenty-one. The round resumed like nothing happened after he settled back in, grinning when declared the winner. If he had to sit and wait, it only felt natural to enjoy himself.

Walks In Shadow left the saloon while Clint hustled the locals out of their money. It was nice to see him acting like himself again. Roy's orders to wait until a guilty party was found made sense, but inaction never sat right with him and his partner. Luckily, the things that brought them joy were both nearby and plentiful.

The moon sat overhead, saturated in yellow like a jaundiced infant. He let himself meld into the darkness, his form invisible to all, save himself. He moved with the swift certainty of a cat, closing in on his destination in complete quiet. The brothel towered over him, two stories tall and constructed of rough lumber. He walked to the front door and pressed himself tightly against the wall.

After waiting a few minutes, the door opened. A patron swaggered past, soaked in carnal contentment. Walks took advantage, slipping past him, unseen, inside the whorehouse. While the building's exterior held a coarse appearance, the inside drowned in trappings of wealth and elegance.

Black and gold Damascus covered every wall, oil nudes hung in equidistant places throughout the space. He crept up a stairwell on the right side of the room, his loins stirring with each step. A narrow hallway stretched out before him at the top of the stairs, doors lining either side. Walks rubbed his hands together, a wolfish grin upon his face that none could see. It was time to choose his entertainment for the night.

By the fifth hand Clint had won, all the men at the table had left and been replaced by fresh suckers. Well—all but one. The gnarled old man sat hunched over his cards with an enraged look plastered upon his heavily lined face. An eyepatch covered his right eye, the left flitting from his hand to Clint repeatedly.

He ignored the geriatric's glare, playing through the round without comment. His number in this hand was eighteen, and like each time before, he paused time to work the cards in his favor. As the dealer declared him the winner, the old man abruptly rose to his feet and slammed his hands on the tabletop.

"Yer a goddamn cheat, mister!" he shouted, his remaining eye bulging in unbridled rage. Clint smirked, his steely eyes locking with his accuser's. He stood, removing his coat and rolling back his sleeves.

"Ain't no hidden cards on me, old man. I suggest you leave now, before I crack your fucking skull with my bare hands."

The elderly gambler stepped backward, looking around for someone, *anyone* who would have his back. Upon the realization that no one did, he turned and left the saloon in a huff. The other men at the table remained silent. Clint's rekindled aggression waned over the following round, which he lost on purpose to dash suspicions. He rose, tipped his hat to the saps he'd bled dry, and walked upstairs to his room. He kicked off his dusty black boots and sank into the bed. Sleep came soon after.

Walks In Shadow held his cock in a death grip in the corner of a cramped bedroom. A whore the size of a tugboat lay on her belly, rolls overlapping either side of the mattress. Her john was a scrawny man with broken teeth and greasy, dark hair. He rubbed his pecker up and down the dark and mottled trench between her legs. After a few drunken jabs, the filthy yokel plunged his modest cock into her drooling chasm.

The whore took him, emitting a low, husky moan. Her matted pubic mound glistened in the viscous discharge as her cunt wept. Walks sniffed deeply, taking in the rancid bouquet formed by the reek of their fluids and unwashed genitals. Their rutting was beautiful—mounds of fat rolling like the tides of the sea—the air thick and damp from their heat. Sweet release drew near, his balls aching for resolution.

The john pulled loose of her pussy with a wet, sucking sound. Air released from her gash, the queef causing her mudflaps to undulate. He buried his ratty face between her turd-cutters, lapping her o-ring like a thirsty dog. He pursed his lips around her shitter and sucked hard. A gout of watery shit gushed from her puckered hole, splashing the man's face and chest. He began to lick and suck up the scat, and Walks In Shadow shot a huge load onto the floor.

Walks released his cloak once he was well and clear of the brothel. Despite the empty streets and silence, he felt a minor flash of dread in the air. He walked back toward Wrangler's Rest, an eerie fog clinging to the land. The whiskey in his blood and orgasm had left him utterly exhausted. He walked through the double doors of the saloon, and as they clapped shut behind him, he thought he heard a scream off in the distance. He shrugged it away and went up to his room for the night.

7

LUCANOS

S atan's son stood before a sacrificial altar carved from black stone. A bawling infant writhed atop the slab, tears streaming its pink face. He gazed upon the damned child in utter disinterest, running a slender thumb across the dagger in his hand. His pale skin split at the blade's point, stitching back together almost instantly.

Lucanos plunged the dagger into the child's soft spot, the blade hitting its spine at the other end. It cried no more, its motions halted by death's embrace. Blood pooled beneath the postpartum abortion, collecting in carved runes atop the altar. He pulled his blade free, coated in blood and tiny gray flecks of brain.

A green glow engulfed the stone slab. The infant curled in on itself, disintegrating into a small pile of ashes. It would regenerate elsewhere—one of millions of children that God did not claim, damned for eternity. The energy converted into a beam atop the altar, blasting upward toward Earth. Lucanos grinned at the sight, and ran his forked tongue over the dagger, cleaning off the remaining blood and flesh.

Like his father, he bore mostly angelic features, save for his mouth and eyes. They were serpent traits, inherent to the denizens of Inferno. This sacrifice, like all the ones before, caused his slitted pupils to expand in ecstasy. Unbeknownst to the peons of Murrayville, the last kill had been set in motion by his blood magick. He laughed in melodic snatches, his silk finery billowing as he turned to exit the blood chamber.

For too long, mankind had gotten by unscathed from Hell's fire. Their ledger would be paid in full, and *soon*. His father gave Adam a choice and was denied paradise for it. The children of Christ would plead on bleeding knees for mercy and receive none. Lucanos pondered the future while six of his concubines lapped and sucked on his thorned cock.

Their tongues probed his ass and balls, lips caressing every inch of his enormous, scaly appendage. His mind drifted to sights of his dominion on Earth. Flames consumed their pathetic structures, daemons raping and slaughtering people out in the streets. Humanity's toll would make God weep atop his shiny little throne. Earth would fall, and Heaven after.

The tongue in his ass slid deeper, warm and wet pressure summoning a heady flow of green pre-cum. The sluts slurped it dutifully as an orgasm built up. Lucanos felt his ascension approaching both on Earth and in his bedchambers. He saw himself adorned in the dress of a king, a crown of thorns atop his head. The sheep bowed before him with their noses pressed to the dirt—and Lucifer's spawn came into his whores' mouths.

The Well of Torment was nigh.

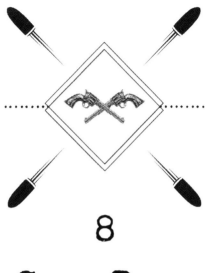

8

GRIM DAWN

P anicked screams arrived with the sun's dawning. Clint abruptly rose, bolting downstairs and out onto the street. People lined the main strip, clustered in front of businesses with terror-stricken faces. He squinted in the direction they all faced, noting the silhouetted shape of a man. Walks In Shadow approached and stood beside him, his bow in hand.

The shape moved slowly, limbs twitching and motions erratic. It dragged its limbs as it moved, kicking up clouds of dust in its path. Terrified shrieks rang out, following its procession like a rolling wave of sound. Then—the shape became defined, and Clint felt a surge of shock.

A flayed man lurched on bloody feet, muscles gleaming redly under the raging sun. His skinned cock swayed with his motions, blood dripping down and blackening the yellow soil. The cadaver's lower jaw hung loosely. Its one eye rocked side-to-side in jarring twitches. It halted before the church and turned to face the townsfolk.

A smile spread across the aberration's face as it parted skinless lips to speak.

"Abandon all hope, ye sheep of Christ's flock. The Dragon of the Abyss arrives on the morrow. This world shall crumble beneath Hell's might. Lucanos will take your children into his harem and pump them full of his wicked seed. You shall all—"

BLAM!

The talking corpse's head exploded into meaty chunks. It fell backwards to the ground, its hellish un-life put to an end. Sheriff Gallagher stood, smoke billowing from the barrel of his Colt .44. He holstered his revolver and ordered for the body to be hauled off.

Father O'Leary lay curled in the fetal position behind the pulpit. The voices had returned, and sooner than expected. They had called and compelled him for over a month, their song darkly irresistible. Prayer and his rosary could not abate their malevolent sway.

His orders began with miserly tasks, like painting pentagrams onto houses, or placing small idols about town. Soon after, the voices called for blood. He remembered flaying the skin from Claire's sumptuous tits, then slitting her belly and admiring the intestinal coils that dangled. The best part had been raping her as she died with a massive wooden cross. He had jammed it to its crossbeams in her hairy, juicy gash and admired the blood.

He wept, his visions bathed in a sadism that was not his. Patrick's short, brown hair sat in disarray, his eyes reddened by tears. A schism cleaved his soul in twain—his piety in ruination before Hell's unshakeable hold. The voices grew louder, darker memories flooding his already tortured mind.

Two orphans—one boy, one girl—forced to fuck at gunpoint. The boy sobbed and begged his sister's forgiveness as he thrust himself deeply into her. O'Leary slit their throats during the act. He wrapped their bodies in barbed wire and left them displayed in their final act of incestuous coitus for the world to see. The priest wept, though his cock stood erect beneath black trousers.

One soul remains owed to your patron, the voices hissed.

Patrick shook his head fervently, crying a mantra of repeated 'no's. He knew his protests made little difference. This had been his fate from the moment he'd succumbed to darkness.

The voices grew louder and more incessant, his head aching in a rhythmic throb. He drew up to his knees, the surrounding church dim and devoid of the holy spirit he once praised. Father O'Leary produced a straight razor from a pants pocket with a trembling hand. His internal choir screamed ravenously as damnation drew near.

Outside, he heard screams, which halted his efforts. Moments later, the thunderous pop of a pistol rang out. All drew to an apex—he felt the tides of fate shifting like angry tectonic plates. The voices blurred on, their tempo and volume verging on madness. He rolled his sleeves back, sweat pouring down his form in nervous streams.

Considering his many transgressions against God, what was but one parting sin? The first cut went deep, skin and muscle parting beneath the blade like the Red Sea. Patrick gasped and switched hands. Blood flowed from his wrist to the inner crook of his elbow in sanguine sheets. He slit his other forearm wide open and fell backward onto the wooden floor.

Father O'Leary grew cold. Warm blood pooled beneath him. The voices no longer shouted, but were silent. Then, as death fell over Lucanos' pawn—they laughed. His soul departed his body, and his final thoughts were that he'd made a grave mistake.

9

WELL, WELL, WELL—

A rumbling began in the ground. It started in the desert beyond Murrayville's outskirts, drawing in slowly, like the steps of an awakened deity. Cracks formed on the earth, reaching further and further towards the doomed folk who dwelled there. The fractures grew deeper and swifter, running down the road that bisected the town.

While most slipped free of the perilous chasms, a few were not so fortunate. They slipped under; the earth snapping shut as the cracks ran ever forward. Around the church, the ground shook violently as the fissures converged. The house of God trembled before Satan's wrath.

Windows exploded gouts of shattered glass outward, the wooden boards groaning from the tremulous soil below. Then—it collapsed. Sands churned, devouring every remaining trace of the chapel. Black stone bubbled upward, shifting and morphing as it rose from the depths.

The liquid obsidian took form, expanding outward, until, at last, the Well of Torment stood. It was a gargantuan construct with cruelly barbed hooks jutting out at quadrilateral points. A green glow encased the well, its dark power audibly thrumming. Though it could not speak, it called for souls.

People scattered in all directions, the air dense in terror. Overhead, the sun went red. A slitted pupil formed in its center, the star now a serpent's eye. It flitted side-to-side, observing the panicked mob below. Sheriff Gallagher barked orders over the din, seizing control of the desperate situation.

Motes of blue light appeared over spots where the ground had swallowed people up. They floated lackadaisically through the air, siphoned by the well's irresistible pull. Five luminous specks drifted toward it, then went in and vanished from sight. Moments later, forks of green lightning belched skyward, the air hissing angrily.

Irving Stetman, the local gunsmith, rolled out a Gatling gun and parked it on the road. Sheriff Gallagher ordered for everyone to take up fighting positions and took his spot behind the death machine with his hand on its crank. Clint and Walks In Shadow took their places on either side of the street with their weapons drawn. Every armed person stood ready.

A sound echoed up angrily from the depths of the well. It grew louder and more defined with repetition. The bleeding sky raged above, and before too long, it became apparent what the sound was:

Flap, flap, flap—

A winged creature rising from hell. A bloodbath was imminent.

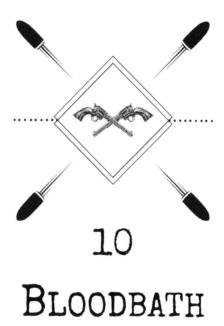

10

BLOODBATH

The silence before battle shrouded all in its oppressive smog. Clint counted the seconds between each beating wing, his Colts drawn and heart racing. Sheriff Roy looked down the barrels of the Gatling gun with sweat streaming down his face. On and on, the wings flapped—louder and louder as the daemon drew near.

"I don't give two shits about wasting ammunition, men! Y'all see an ugly cunt from hell, you shoot that cocksucker until it's good and dead! Do I make myself clear?!" Roy shouted. War cries greeted his orders.

Flap...flap...flap...

Satan's eye watched all from on high. Clint flinched despite himself every time he caught sight of it. The flapping halted—and all sounds ceased. An air-shattering BOOM ripped from the well as a dark blur exited like a cannonball.

"OPEN FIRE!"

Gunshots cracked the air, the winged beast screeching overhead. It burst upward on massive, leathery wings. Clint caught sight of it just before it disappeared into the crimson skies. Daemons flooded from the well, all scaly, horned abominations. Their skin was a blackish-red, their faces flat with slitted nostrils and serpent's eyes. Sheriff Gallagher cranked the Gatling, unloading lead into the swarm. They fell into a heap, all of Murrayville laying down fire with reckless abandon.

Although the ground invaders were a threat, Clint felt more concerned about the aerial wretch hiding in the clouds. He scanned for the high-flier's return with wide eyes. If it was directly overhead, he couldn't hear it over the gunfire. Blood and innards lay at the foot of the well. Daemon corpses were turned into mincemeat by high-caliber hatred. Suddenly, a man screamed from one of the rooftops.

Clint looked up just in time to glimpse him before the flying beast whisked him away. His wails continued—then halted abruptly. Blood's rich iron doused the air, his body tossed down in brutalized halves. It plummeted into the orange soil, exploding into chunks of viscera on impact.

Green lightning hissed from the Well of Torment again, followed by a fresh flood of Hellspawn to the slaughter. Wretched faces exploded under the barrage, misting the air with blood. Clint fired into the fray, though he kept vigilant for the flier's re-appearance. Right on cue, another man yelped from a rooftop to his left.

He motioned at Walks In Shadow with a plan forming in his mind. Walks ran across the road to him, leaning in so he could hear him over the surrounding chaos.

"That flying cunt up top ain't helping matters," Clint said.

"Agreed. What do you propose we do?"
Clint told his partner about the plan. Walks In Shadow nodded assent to his strategy, then vanished. It was time for the Loathsome Two to get to work.

Clint stood on the general store's rooftop. He felt vulnerable, like a mongoloid caught with his dick in his hand. Regardless of his feelings, he knew the risk was necessary. The winged daemon had yet to resurface, though the man still screamed in its dark embrace within the churning nimbus. Like before, the sky-plucked lad stopped screaming and returned to earth in two pieces.

In defiance of every protesting cell in his body, Clint shouted at the sky.

"You ever get drilled in the ass by a real man?! I reckon I can show you what eight inches of hard Texan cock feels like if you're curious! Come on down, bat-bitch!"

An ear-piercing roar ripped down from the sky in response. Clint felt every hair on his body standing on end, his eyes scanning for movement. If he wanted to survive this, his timing had to be *perfect*. Cheating at cards and killing creatures from hell were two distinct skill sets entirely.

Clint felt the wind from the daemon's powerful wings before he saw it. It shot toward him with fangs bared.

Just before it landed its vicious tackle, his eyes glowed. Time slowed, the monster suspended mid-flight. Walks In Shadow appeared, hopping onto its back and pulling a knife free of his boot. The native's teeth clenched, his blade summoning gouts of dark blood from the monster's throat with each slice. Skin yielded to muscle, then bone.

Clint felt his grip on time loosening, a throb forming in his temple. The daemon collapsed to the roof, Walks lifting its severed head high and letting blood pour onto him with a blood-thirsty grin.

"Fun ain't over yet!" Clint shouted with glee. He turned and fired into the swarming throng. Muzzles flared wherever the eye could see. Gunsmoke hung thick over the battlefield Murrayville had become.

The Loathsome Two picked daemons off from the rooftop while grinning. Every shot fired added to the midden heap of hell-sent soldiers around the well. They fell with undignified cries of pain, blood pooling beneath their mangled corpses. Moments that felt like eternal dirges elapsed as the men battled on.

Although fear nearly crippled them, combat had exposed an edge to the people of Murrayville. Clint saw it in their eyes: a murderous gleam and willingness to stand and fight. It gave him hope—a dangerous thing in the times he faced.

The final dregs of the hell-sent raid fell, bloodied and broken. For a long time after the last shot rang out, no one spoke. The men all departed for their homes. For now, it seemed Murrayville could catch its breath. Satan's eye watched them, keeping vigil for the death yet to come.

11

RIFT-GATE

While the citizens of Murrayville grasped what little rest they could, Lucanos seethed in his bedchamber. One hundred daemons, including a Sergeant—and hardly a dent made. His harem lay about his bedchamber in bloodied pieces. Bits of flesh and blood still clung to his barbed manhood. They'd regenerate and return, of course, but likely with less vigor in their carnal endeavors. Trauma had that effect on people, from his experience.

All was not lost, of course. Not by a long shot. He strolled from the chamber and through winding corridors of ebony stone. Guttering skull-torches aligned the passageways, bathing the hallways in flickering light. His alabaster complexion reflected the luminance, his eyes slitted in annoyance. Each footfall echoed soft patterings throughout the causeways he traversed.

If his forces couldn't seize the foothold he sought, it was time to get involved. He turned at an intersection of passageways and entered the scrying chamber. A font brimming with metallic liquid sat at the center of the dim room. Lucanos stood over it and sliced his palm with a sharp nail. A single droplet of blood fell into the pool, which emanated a red glow.

Visions blurred by, all captured by the sky sentry he'd placed over Murrayville. To the simpletons, it must have been a terrifying sight. Lucanos cackled at their fear-pinched faces, enjoying the tangible unrest among the flock. He watched the battle unfold—a storm of lead, a tangle of daemon limbs as bullets tore his forces asunder. The Sergeant wreaked havoc from above, his violence summoning a smirk upon Lucanos' face.

Uthblek brought its prey above the clouds, wrenching them in half with taloned hands. Their intestines slopped out like overcooked noodles. Each piece of their ruined bodies plummeted below, impacting upon the ground with satisfying splats and explosions of blood. All of his reverie halted at the next sight he beheld.

A cowboy clad in black taunted his sergeant from a rooftop. It descended for the attack, then—his sky sentry's feed of vision went black. When it returned, his sergeant lay beheaded and gloated over by both the gunslinger and another man Lucanos hadn't noticed before.

How'd he get there so quickly?, he thought.

The report he'd received from his lieutenant omitted the pair he now looked upon. They were a problem—one he'd rectify the moment an opportunity presented itself. He left the scrying chamber to get dressed, with a plan developing in his mind.

Lucanos and the Whore of Babylon stood outside the rift-gate. A red silk dress draped down her ample body, shoulder-length black curls framing a moon-shaped face with blue eyes and full lips. Her gaze was hollow, for no soul dwelled within. Though time was pressing, the sight of her sent a stirring through his loins.

"I've need of your mouth, slut."

"I exist to serve, on knees or back, my prince."

She lowered herself, tugging Lucanos silk trousers down. His throbbing member sprang free, bouncing upward and casting a wide shadow across her pale, upturned face. She lapped his balls, tenderly sucking each into her mouth and massaging them with a deft tongue. Her hands massaged his pulsing shaft while she gazed up in adoration.

Lucanos released a low moan and let his body relax. The Whore gently released his testicles from her mouth and ran her tongue up the underside of his reptilian phallus, tracing fat veins in worship. Her mouth tore at the corners, muscle gleaming through as blood flowed in warm, sticky trickles. She paid the pain no heed, pumping and embracing his size with the wet softness of her throat.

"Father did his best work when he made you," he crooned.

Climax approached, her efforts doubling in speed and passion as his muscles tensed. Blood ran down her chin and her throat swelled with each thrust. Lucanos growled, erupting a heavy flood of seed into her esophagus. She sucked until she'd swallowed every thick and salty drop.

"You've done well. Rise and let us set forth, my slave. Hell is due souls."

Lucanos and the Whore of Babylon walked toward the rift-gate, a black archway covered in spikes that glowed green. He took one last look at his father's kingdom. If all went well, heaven's army wouldn't even notice that he'd broken the pact before it was too late. They stepped through the portal.

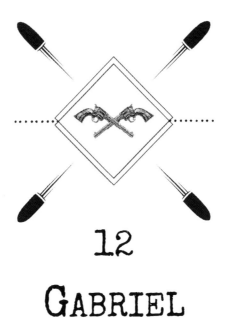

12

GABRIEL

C lint couldn't sleep after the excitement of repelling hell's soldiers. Considering the odds they'd faced, he felt they'd done damn good. Luck was no negligible factor in the victory, either. He pondered his life, marveling at the path given to him. In a million years, he'd never have guessed this was where he'd ended up. He sat upright on the narrow bed and lit a cigarette. A sadness hung over him in the waning hours of the night.

The Loathsome Two had done many bad things in their lives. Too many to count, in fact. Gabriel must have known these days approached when he met them. Even so—why had *they*, of all people, been chosen in this war between heaven and hell? Each development only brought more questions. Clint grabbed a fifth of whiskey from the nightstand beside him and up-ended it. Despite all he'd drank, memories of Mexico came flooding back.

The Juarez Bloodriders were a terrible outfit to ride alongside, but their bounty payouts were too good to resist. Clint and Walks In Shadow worked with them for months, gunning down killers and innocents, alike. None of that phased Clint. In fact, the rush of the kill had him in its clutches like an opium addiction. In those days of indiscriminate barbarism, the stakes raised with each job they completed. They pursued increasingly dangerous gangs, until, at last, the Dominguez gang were in their sights.

Wanted for over three hundred counts of murder, two hundred and thirty-nine counts of rape, and one hundred and eighty-six counts of robbery, each Dominguez gang member was worth a small fortune. Clint and Walks had drooled over the substantial figure, especially considering the gang hosted twenty-two members. The pair agreed to aid in one last bounty before departing north to deposit their earnings. They rode west—fifteen men crossing brutal and unforgiving desert.

For two weeks, they traveled in silence with eyes squinted against the blazing sun. On their fifteenth day, they arrived at a small town with no name. Adobe houses sprawled across the space. Chickens roamed freely while people tended gardens, worked, or hawked simple, well-made goods. Clint felt a small amount of peace there. The pueblo was a stark contrast to the land they'd crossed to get there.

Alejandro Juarez, head of the Bloodriders, asked around for information regarding their quarry while everyone else watered their horses and rested in the shade. He returned an hour later with a grin on his sand-scoured face.

"Rest up, men. Our bounties are only about ten miles north of here. Apparently, the Dominguez boys have themselves a nice little commune near a river. We ride at sunset," he said. Everyone nodded, grateful for the small reprieve after so much hard traveling. Clint lit a smoke and took a pull from his flask. He smiled peacefully, unaware that his life was about to change forevermore.

The Bloodriders slowed their horses to a slow trot a mile out from their target. Moonlight filtered through the sparse trees, nighttime insects filling the uneasy silence. A large shape emerged from the shadows ahead. Alejandro raised a fist to call for a halt. Everyone dismounted and went forth on foot, armed and bristling for action.

Walks In Shadow scouted ahead, crouched low and near silent. By the time the other bounty hunters caught up, four men lay dead around the perimeter with slit throats. Clint and the others cleared the surrounding area, then huddled around Alejandro in the treeline. He spoke in a low voice while his eyes darted around in search of movement.

"Carlito, Julio—block the door up. Doesn't have to be perfect, just enough to slow them down. Everyone else, grab a torch. We'll light these bastards up."

So they did, their brands igniting the house and beginning to spread. Boards soon crackled, the fire devouring the structure as smoke rose into the star-lit sky. Screams erupted from within the home as the flames grew more ravenous.

Those trapped in the burning building beat on the door frantically. The Bloodriders guffawed while Clint and Walks stood in grim silence. The screams reached a fevered pitch, and the door finally gave way under pummeling fists. People flooded across the threshold in a sea of cooking flesh. Burnt hair filled the air with its putrid stench while vocal cords cooked. Clint laughed with the rest of the men—until a child no older than five stumbled outside, bathed in flames.

The only course of action that came to mind was putting the little one out of her misery. He lifted a Colt, and was interrupted by Alejandro shouting, "Don't waste the bullet! Let her burn!" The Bloodriders' laughter felt more like an icepick to the brain with each ugly peal. Clint felt something crumble inside of himself. In light of such evil, his humanity stirred.

He locked eyes with Walks for a moment, then opened fire. The girl collapsed mercifully with his first bullet. Neither Alejandro nor his underlings noticed when the Loathsome Two turned and began to shoot at them. Clint's first shot caught Carlito in the throat. He fell to his knees, gurgling weakly while arterial blood sprayed in crimson arcs.

Walks felled two Bloodriders with quick and well-aimed arrows to the back. They fell over screaming, never to rise again. The partners let loose, bullets and arrows dropping men like flies. Then only Alejandro remained. Clint fired off another shot, and his revolvers clicked impotently. The Mexican leered, raising his rifle in his direction. Just as his finger slid into the trigger well, his right eye burst forth from his skull, impaled upon an arrow.

The Loathsome Two both collapsed on their asses, covered in blood and panting. Clint's hands were tremulous, his eyes wide from the chaos. Everything had changed—they both felt it, though it wouldn't be said aloud. Their bounties were charred husks, and they'd just killed the one man officials trusted to verify their identities.

A light flared in the darkened heavens above. They gazed upon it in exhausted silence, watching it trek through infinite spaces beyond their reach. It descended at great speeds—like a falling star, though it held a far greater luminance. Clint shielded his eyes from the scalding brightness. When he could no longer see the light beaming through his hands, he lowered them.

The gunslinger felt an overwhelming sense of awe at what lay before him and his partner. An angel towered over them, its skin alight with a supernatural radiance. The heavenly soldier wore gilded armor, long auburn hair framing a face too perfect to be human. Massive white wings sat upon its shoulders, its eyes like infinitely deep sapphires set into a marble sculpture.

The Loathsome Two couldn't speak in the celestial being's powerful presence. They sat, gazing upon the archangel with shocked expressions. Every hair on Clint's body stood on end. Then he spoke in a deep and commanding voice.

"Gaze upon me, and know that I am Gabriel—Archangel of the High Heavens, and the right hand of God. On this day, I grant you both a boon: my blood. May it aid you in your days to come."

Though questions ran amuck in his mind, Clint could only sit in reverential silence. Gabriel stepped forward and placed a pale hand on his head. Jolts of pleasure and pain surged throughout his body. Neurons ignited, his arteries expanding and contracting at exponentially increasing speeds. When the archangel lifted his hand, he collapsed while panting. Walks In Shadow received his gift in much the same way.

Before departing, he left them with a message.

"You will ponder why I've given my blood to you. It is a natural response for those of your ilk. I will say only this: a time may come where the innocent reach out to you for aid. Heed that call."

As quickly as he had appeared, Gabriel was gone.

Clint drunkenly slammed the empty bottle down on his nightstand. He looked across the room to find an empty bed. Knowing Walks, he was out blowing loads. He grimaced, laying his head down. Thunder rolled overhead, but he gradually fell asleep. Hidden in the storm, a lone bolt of lightning shot upward in the distance.

JAMES FISHER

13

IN VINO VERITAS

Lucanos and the Whore emerged from the well with
a dark sky overhead and roars of thunder echoing
across the desolate plains in the distance. He bid her to
follow, walking unhurriedly across the main road and between two shops. Breaching the pact by entering earth
wouldn't go without notice for long in heaven. Lesser
daemons were allowed their fun, but *never* arch daemons.
With that in mind, he intended to make the most of the
time afforded to him.

They traipsed through shadows, turning right once they were clear of the alleyway. Dry ground spit dust upwards underfoot, but nary a particle clung to Lucanos' silk garb. With his destination in sight, he picked up his pace. Murrayville Orphanage stood on an acre of barren land, a ramshackle wooden fence enclosing its backyard. The Whore rushed ahead and held the door for him with a curtsey. He entered, a grin spreading across his face.

The orphanage was fairly clean, a hallway with doors aligning either side stretching beyond the foyer in which he stood. The first door on the right opened with a creak, an elderly woman emerging with glazed-over eyes. She shuffled toward him, her silver hair disheveled and hanging in greasy and frayed clumps. Her navy cotton dress was heavily stained and soiled. She bowed to him, then rose and remained mute.

"Have you tended my flock as I bid you, old one?"

"Yes, dark prince. They're all accounted for and resting in their beds."

"Good. Rouse them and instruct them to stand by. Slave, you're to gather what knowledge you can on the two mortals who slew Uthblek."

The Whore of Babylon bowed before departing to fulfill his wishes. Lucanos made himself comfortable in a bedroom prepared for him at the end of the hallway. He held a vintage cabernet on his nightstand, clamping the cork between his teeth and wresting it loose with a loud pop. Its taste was dry and sumptuous. He swigged it back and smiled. It was *damn* good to be royalty.

Babylon's whore walked slowly through the town, her eyes missing nothing, even in the darkness. She peeked in the windows of homes, always listening for voices or clues. After an hour, she'd mostly seen people sleeping, aside from one home. She watched a couple in the throes of passion through their bedroom window. Though she had urgent matters elsewhere, she could not resist touching herself before moving on.

After temporarily quelling her gargantuan libido, she set back to her task. Each home was much the same, people sleeping fitfully, and none of them her intended quarry. She worked row-by-row until she reached businesses aligning the left side of the road. It had been two hours, and now that the storm had diminished some, she saw deputies patrolling. She slunk against the backsides of shops, peering through windows where she could.

Onward she went, searching high and low. She pressed herself to the sides of buildings whenever she feared being seen. The last structure sat a distance away from the others, two stories tall and with no windows. The Whore crept through shadows toward it, a ray of light jutting through the front door when she was less than a stone's throw away. She hid, making herself small and holding her breath as he walked near. He passed by without incident, reeking of sex and sin. Her cunt drooled, the knowledge that she stood outside a brothel rousing the slumbering beast within.

Like a moth to flame, she was compelled to enter. Whether she learned anything relevant was of little import, considering the lust so fundamental to her being. She stood fully upright, smoothing her dress with her hands before walking in.

JAMES FISHER

By the time Lucanos finished his bottle of wine, the silver-haired wretch stood silently outside his doorway. He rose from the bed on which he sat, roughly shouldering his way past her with no remark. Six children stood in a neat line in the hallway with vacant expressions. He sneered, eyeing them contemptuously.

"My sheep, it is time for you to serve your purpose. Grab an ax and set forth. Destroy every carriage or wagon you find. Slay their horses and mules. If anyone should try to stop you—bury your blade in their skull."

The brats departed silently, each grabbing an ax from a small pile by the doorway before slipping into the darkness. Lucanos took a moment to relish the brewing violence at his behest. Much suffering would come from his words, the power an intoxicant to his prideful mind. He looked at the slouching crone still standing outside his door, with a wonderful idea forming.

"Old one, bring me rope and meet me in the kitchen."

"As you wish, dark prince," she replied hollowly before bowing and walking away. He stood there upon her return, his clothes in a neatly folded pile atop a nearby counter. She handed him a coil of rope, then stared at nothing with her arms hanging limply at her sides.

"Strip down and show me your long tits, you fucking cow," he hissed.

82

The walking invalid complied, shrugging weathered shoulders and letting her dress fall to her feet. Her body inspired both excitement and disgust, her breasts hanging to her naval over a wrinkled and pooching belly. Nipples darker than mud and thicker than a thumb jutted out at their crests, cross-eyed and hard in the nighttime chill.

"Lay on the table, cunt."

She promptly obeyed, providing him with a generous view of her sagging asscheeks and dangling pussy lips as she stiffly climbed atop the table. Once in position, she lay perfectly still while staring at the ceiling. Lucanos bound her to the table, her skin red and fat jutting in mounds from the great tension. Once she was well-secured, he let dark ideas flit through his mind while idly stroking his cock.

Something occurred to him while he plotted: a willing victim provided little pleasure. With her usefulness expired, the blood magick binding her was no longer needed. He held a hand over her face and commanded her to open her mouth. A single drop of blood fell onto her tongue from his slit palm.

Her eyes lost their absent quality almost instantly, fear quickly sweeping across her features.

"Wh-what's happening? Who are you, and where are the children?!" she shrieked. Lucanos slapped her across the mouth, her head whipping to the side as blood and spittle sprayed. She softly whimpered, tears roaming the craggy valleys of her aged face. He laughed, grabbing the wine bottle he'd drained from the countertop and walking to the foot of the table.

"Fret not for the children, for you face a far worse fate than they. As for who I am and what's happening? I am Lucanos, and the world is ending by my hand."

With no further ado, he climbed astride her with the bottle in hand. Her cries and pleas were little more than the buzzing of a gnat to his ears as violence drew perilously near. He tenderly probed her gray-tufted nethers with the mouth of the bottle, tracing delicate lines up and down her rancid cleft. He slid the neck inside slowly, his wrist pumping with increasing speed. Before too long, creamy discharge clung to the glass, the stench akin to a barrel full of rotten fish and expired milk.

"Oh, enjoying ourselves, are we? FUCKING SLUT!" he bellowed. Lucanos jerked his wrist at a severe angle, the bottle's neck snapping off inside of her. She wailed and thrashed in her bindings. Her twat menstruated blood, glass, and ribbons of shredded birth canal. His laughter boomed, pinching her clitorus with his free hand between sharply nailed fingers and pulling it taut. The nerve cluster sliced off easily with the ruined bottle, coming free in less than three hacks. He popped the pink bit of flesh into his mouth, savoring it before swallowing.

Her pain sang to him, her blood and flesh an exquisite treat. Lucanos aligned his deadly phallus with her bleeding gash and thrust all the way to the hilt. She convulsed and drooled like a rabid animal, her gut expanding and contracting with the outline of his size. Something inside of her ruptured from his hate-fucking—blood pouring in unabashed torrents down his testicles and thighs. Release came like a tidal wave, his dick withdrawing, slick in fluids. Blood and cum oozed from her butchered orifice, her throat raw from screaming.

He dismounted her and walked to the head of the table so that he could look her in the eyes while she died.

"Don't be too sad. Though you die alone here, you'll have plentiful company in hell." She screamed weakly as he brought the remaining half of the ruined bottle down onto her face. Skin sheared, eyeballs bursting with yellowish jelly with each slash. Her body went limp long before he was finished. Brain dripped from her decimated skull, her head hewn into pieces from the nose up.

Lucanos dressed himself, dropping what little remained of the ruined bottle to the floor. He grabbed a fresh bottle from a rack on the kitchen's back wall and went to his bedroom. He couldn't help but bask in the afterglow of his barbarism between gulps of wine. More daemons would soon enter the fray, his only hope that the Whore found something useful soon.

14

BLADE IN THE DARK

After such an action-packed day, Walks In Shadow couldn't sleep. Naturally, he went to the brothel again. After peeping through keyholes, he found a sight that enticed him more than the others. He slipped into the room, his dick shifting down his thigh. He hadn't noticed this whore previously, but now he couldn't look away. His unseen eyes locked upon her in adoration.

The midget straddled an old man's face, her ass like two plump hams. They jiggled with her grinding motions. Her cum ran clear rivers down his cheeks, all silent in the room aside from the wet sounds of him lapping her cunt like a thirsty dog. Walks stroked himself slowly, taking in the ample curves of her slight frame. A lustful gasp nearly escaped his lips at the sight of her twisting her nipples while feeding the old-timer juices.

Red curls cascaded down the pale slope of her arched back, eyes like blazing emeralds. Even the little gap between her front teeth drove him wild, his balls aching to flood her with seed and make her his. She let out a sudden moan, her thighs aquiver, delicious rippling waves rolling across her lower body. She rose, the man gasping for air, her juicy slit gushing in spurts like a waterfall. Her ejaculate shot across the room, slaps to her pussy causing fresh surges of euphoria.

Walks slowed his hand just before going over the edge. He watched her slide down, squatting over the man's member and taking it into her tight, pink asshole. She glided down with a low moan, his cock now balls deep. He wanted to know what it felt like inside her, to fill her holes, to watch her upturned face as she licked his sack and tugged on his manhood. But he didn't want to buy her for a night. He wanted something he'd never desired before: commitment.

It didn't take long for his control to crumble away. Just as the compact goddess rose to finish the john off, he spurted, barely able to remain quiet from the overwhelming pleasure. Walks quietly slipped away, making his way down the stairs with images of the red-haired beauty seared into his brain. He noticed a strange woman upon reaching the foot of the stairs.

A red dress flowed down her voluptuous body, out of place for a town like Murrayville. Although she was beautiful, something seemed amiss. Her eyes held no light, her expression flat and lifeless. A prospective client for the brothel stood before her, engaged in crass and charmless conversation. Walks In Shadow watched, noting how little she emoted during their chat. It was as though her tether to humanity had been severed.

The brothel's proprietor walked toward them from his office in the back, heavy footfalls and labored pants announcing his arrival before his massive gut rounded the corner and into Walks' field of vision.

"Good evenin', Kurt. Who's this we're speaking to? Sure don't look like one of my gals."

"I don't think she is, Rhett, but I'm certainly willing to pay for a spin." The greasy man chuckled at his own wit, the big man's face rapidly going beet-red.

"If she ain't on my staff, you do that shit somewhere else! Get the fuck out of here!" he shouted, shooing them away while sweat poured down his bloated face. The strange woman and idiot left. Something about her urged Walks to follow and observe.

Deputy Crenshaw walked his patrol route, fear cold and heavy in his gut. Although he understood the importance of monitoring things given the ongoing chaos, he'd much rather be on horseback, well away from there. He kept his eyes peeled, his Colt .45 drawn and ready. The darkened streets of what once was a peaceful town held malice, every shadow a potential threat.

He heard a commotion up ahead, his dawdling walk instantly shifting to an outright sprint. His lantern struggled to keep the darkness at bay, the wind causing its flame to flicker. A diminutive silhouette took form by the weak ray of light his beacon provided. The crunch of steel on wood rang out, the unknown shape bringing an arm up, then down, over and over.

"Halt! What on *earth* are you doing?!" Crenshaw shouted. He stepped forward further still, nearly dropping his lantern at the sight before him. A girl no older than six had completely demolished the Reynolds' wagon, an ax in her hands. Her brown hair clung to a pale face in perspiration-laden strands. The deputy took a few more tentative steps toward the child, noticing the darkness of her eyes, the total inhumanity clinging to her like a chill fog.

"I need you to drop that ax, real quick like. You hear me?! Yer in a world of hurt for destroying property, so I suggest you do what I say—"

An ear-piercing hiss erupted in the distance, interrupting his train of thought. Despite the demented brat in front of him, he couldn't help but turn and stare as green forks of lightning shot upwards from the well across town. Deputy Crenshaw gasped, the growls of daemons echoing across the barren land.

His distraction was rewarded with an ax to the back of his skull. He collapsed, the child braining him with her ax. She struck viciously, gray matter and bone splintering into a ruined puddle, seeping out onto the dry ground.

The girl smiled, turning and walking casually towards the Reynolds' barn with her weapon in tow.

After what seemed an eternity, Walks In Shadow followed the odd duo to a run-down shack on the south side of Murrayville. He kept his steps light and body low to the ground, his mark only five feet away. The man accompanying her drunkenly swayed, pulling a key from a pocket in his filthy trousers. He fumbled with the keyhole on his front door for a moment before the lock clicked. He held the door for his female companion with a salacious leer.

"After you, my lady," he slurred.

"I'm no lady, but I'll never deny a little chivalry," she purred. Her voice was like prickly silk, laden in the shimmering promise of sex. They stepped through the doorway, Walks quickly catching the door before it fully shut. Judging by the horny chuckles trailing away on the other side, he doubted either of the people he trailed would double back to check it. He kneeled for a few moments, listening until he was certain the coast was clear before slipping inside the house.

Roaches scurried underfoot, the furniture all smeared in old food and rat waste. Walks grimaced, the stench a heavy miasma that clung to his skin in an oily film and cloyed at his nostrils. He fought the mouth-watering surge of nausea that flared up, creeping through the dim and narrow hallway. He listened, his instinct taking him to a closed door at the end of the corridor. Low voice murmured on the other side.

Upon peering through the keyhole, Walks In Shadow thought of the best way to get inside without drawing their attention. The woman sat on a dingy bed against the far wall; the man fumbling with his belt at the center of the room. She spoke as he prepared, her tone even and transactional.

"I'll do whatever you desire, so long as you provide the information I seek."

"Shoot—I'll tell you anything you want if you suck my pecker!"

Kurt let a dumb peal of laughter ring out, the woman immune to his abundant charisma. After receiving no accolades for his sharp wit, the drunk continued speaking.

"What do you wanna know?"

"I want everything you can tell me about two bounty hunters who recently came to town. One's a cowboy in all black, the other an Indian. What do you know?"

Walks' pulse quickened at her words, his fists clenched. The man paused, his booze-addled brain straining words sufficient for him to get his dick wet. Then he let out a relieved-sounding gasp.

"Yep! I know the fellers yer talkin' about! The Loathsome Two—that'd be Clint McCoy and Walks In Shadow! As far as I know, they're staying at Wrangler's Rest. I reckon Sheriff Gallagher hired 'em on as extra guns, what with all the hell-business goin' on lately. That's about all I can think of. Is it enough?"

Walks watched the woman rise to her feet and cross the room. She placed her hands on the back of his head, fingers playing with his greasy hair. Full lips parted, her eyes ablaze in lust.

"Yes."

She lowered herself gracefully to her knees, nimble fingers unbuttoning his pants and pulling them down to his ankles. With Kurt's back turned and her view blocked, Walks knew now was the time to get inside the room. He knew not his plan once within, but it beat doing nothing, especially given the exchange he'd just heard. He softly placed his hand on the doorknob, fingers taut as he awaited the perfect moment.

His chance came seconds later, the man moaning loudly in a nasal rasp. Walks In Shadow twisted the doorknob and stepped over the threshold, his pulse hammering in his ears. With deft and subtle motions, he closed the door and slipped past them, settling into an empty corner of the damp and neglected room.

The woman was skilled, no doubt about that. She took the entirety of Kurt's cock down her throat, tongue lapping his musty and hair-covered balls with nary a gag. Her motions were expert, one hand twisting the base of his shaft while the other cupped and caressed his stinky plums. The man panted, his adam's apple bobbing and back arching.

Although the show unfolding before him would typically reignite his libido, Walks could only see that tiny lass with a delectable bottom in his mind's eye. His distraction halted, something strange occurring to the man being sucked off. Small bubbles appeared under his filthy skin, on his hands and feet, rippling back and forth. They moved beneath his flesh like burrowing insects, all converging at his manhood, slurped up by the dutifully sucking slut.

Pained cries replaced lustful elation, Kurt's eyes bulging. His cheeks sunk in, his body rapidly losing mass, crumpling inward like paper. She sucked harder; her moans bestial and tempo unrelenting. He tried to stop her, his shoves and strikes weak and ineffective. Loud cracking sounds filled the room, the man's bones snapping, his body folding in on itself. He collapsed to the floor, his form boneless and reduced to fleshy scraps.

The woman stood, wiping a slimy glob of semen from her cheek with her index finger and licking it up. A dark smile spread across her dead-eyed face. She turned, walking toward the bedroom door and let herself out. Walks wasted no time in closing the gap between himself and her, his knife drawn, the shock of what he'd just witnessed still splashing over him in staticy waves. Just as she reached the front door, he brought the handle of his blade down onto her head with a wet thud.

She fell to the floor in a heap, blood glinting through her hair where he'd struck. Walks In Shadow swept the black locks away that covered her face, scrutinizing her for any sign that she was faking her condition. After twisting her nipples through her dress as hard as he could and receiving no reaction, he was satisfied. With no one left to spot him, he released his cloak and searched the shack for something to secure his prisoner. He found a rope in the ramshackle parlor, returning to her and binding her hands and feet tightly.

With a small grunt, he lifted the unconscious skank and tossed her over his shoulder.

"I hope you're worth all this effort. If not, I'll take great pleasure in fucking you up," he said wistfully. He walked out the front door of the shack with the wretch in tow and made his way toward the sheriff's station. Just as he reached the main road of Murrayville, lightning surged from the well.

"Things don't ever seem to get any easier for us," he pined aloud to himself before sprinting toward the station.

15

FRESH INCURSION

E ven through the veil of sleep, Clint could feel the well activating. He pulled himself to his feet, still dressed. With an exasperated groan, he clamped a cigarette between his teeth and lit it on his way down the stairs. His head pounded, mood soured not only by his interrupted rest, but by the torturous memories that came before. If he had to be awake, the daemons were going to pay heavily for it.

He stepped out onto the main road, thunder roaring in the skies while men took up fighting positions or armed themselves. Irving Stetler prepared the Gatling gun, daubing sweat from his bald head with a red handkerchief while he worked. Clint had yet to spot Roy, so he barked orders to anyone not properly set for engagement. Smoke billowed from his nostrils. He drew his revolvers, cocking the hammers back—a motion more natural to him than swimming was to a fish. The sheriff appeared moments later, striding toward him swiftly.

"Clint."

"Sheriff."

"Walks detained someone. Says she's connected to all this. Her tits tell me she's from heaven, but I've never been a shrewd analyst when it comes to lady folk."

Roy let out a bitter laugh, taking his place behind the mounted gun.

"Should I stand guard on her? You're the one paying me. Just let me know what it is you need seeing to."

Gallagher stroked his silvered mustache, contemplating his following words a bit before responding. The growls of daemons rose in urgency and volume with every passing second.

"No, I need you here. Walks has her in a cell and under watch. We'll see what she has to say if we make it through this."

Clint nodded grimly, spitting his smoke out onto the ground. Roy looked at Irving and asked him if the Gatling was ready and operational. The gunsmith confirmed it was. Every man stood in silence, the battle drawing near. Hisses, grunts, and roars intermingled within the well, nearly deafening. Another peal of thunder boomed across the deserts surrounding Murrayville, and daemons surged upwards from the portal.

Every muzzle flared in the darkness, the first foe's reptilian skull torn asunder by lead. It was quickly replaced by a dozen more red-skinned monstrosities, all glaring and blood-crazed. Clint caught a goat-headed beast between the eyes, then another with the face of a rattlesnake. All around him, men aimed true and fired quickly. Black blood pooled beneath the fallen abominations, skulls hewn or hearts shredded.

The surge of Hellspawn slowly abated, their aggressive push thwarted by townsfolk who'd had their fill of living in fear. Shotguns sawed daemons off at the knees, bullets ripping through skulls and organs. Men let loose primal screams as they held their ground and exerted dominion over the malevolent forces.

Another blast of damnable green arcs shot from the well, halting any premature celebrations like a kick to the balls.

"Don't get your panties in a bunch, men! Keep shooting, and we might make it out of this bullshit alive!" Roy shouted over the gunfire, brows knit and eyes ablaze with a warrior's wrath.

For every daemon felled, another took its place, though the men yielded them no quarter. No winged beast emerged from the well this time, a small blessing, if it could be considered as such. Clint fired until his revolvers clicked, reloading with unnatural speed, his focus unfaltering. Each bullet he sent in the daemon's direction found a home nestled deeply within their brains.

Roy faithfully cranked the Gatling gun, whooping like a cowpoke at his first shindig. Each shot felt like a micro-bomb's detonation, daemons shredded to bloody pulp on the receiving end. The midden heap surrounding the well grew with each shot fired. After the last one fell, Roy rose and ordered everyone to prepare their wagons and horses.

Not ten minutes later, a blustering and heavy-set man returned, shouting in a near-unintelligible drawl. Sheriff Gallagher listened intently, his expression shifting to one of rage.

"FUCK! IF I CATCH WHO DID THIS, I'LL HANG THE COCKSUCKER MYSELF!"

"Roy, what's going on?" Clint asked.

The sheriff turned to face him slowly, red-faced and eyes squinted with unadulterated anger. He leaned close so only the gunslinger could hear—his voice low and seething.

"Someone destroyed every wagon in town. Killed all the fucking mules and horses, too. Follow me to the station. We're gonna have ourselves a little chat with the cunt in the red dress."

16

INTERROGATION

W hen Clint stepped into the station, he saw Walks In Shadow seated at the table, a mostly drank bottle of rye in his hand. They acknowledged one another with a light nod, the room eerily hushed. The woman Roy mentioned lay in the last cell on the left, her hands and feet bound, dark hair swept over her face. He eyed her, enjoying the curves of her body beneath the dirt-stained silk dress.

"Quite a catch you got yourself," he said dryly.

"She's more than she appears. I advise against grabbing yourself a quickie from this one."

"Oh?" Clint responded, taking a seat opposite his friend at the table.

"What can she do? Squirt hard enough to blow a hole through a fellow?"

He began to laugh at his own joke, then halted when he saw that Walks was utterly unamused.

"Much worse, McCoy. Seen her suck the soul out of a man. Before you crack any more jokes, know that I'm not in the fucking mood. She was looking for us. Asked for us by description, in fact. If I hadn't tailed her from the brothel, who knows what she'd have done?"

The gunslinger's initial smirk faded. His jaw clenched as he stood and walked over to her cell.

"Wake up, sleepy tits! You wanted the Loathsome Two, and now you've got us!" he shouted, hammering the bars with clenched fists. After a few more loud raps, she stirred on the wooden bench, expressing her pain in soft whimpers.

Roy stood at his liquor cabinet in the corner, drinking straight from a jar of moonshine. All eyes were upon the woman, her sounds filling the air with a palpable tension. After some struggling, she sat upright, her hands behind her back. The fog over her eyes slowly faded, her features lighting up in recognition.

"Alas! What fortune—to find myself in the company of the men I seek!"

"You clearly know fuck-all about us if you think being our prisoner is fortunate. I have some questions for you. It'd behoove you to answer them, *believe* that," Clint growled. He dragged a chair directly in front of her cell, lighting a cigarette once seated.

"Whatever you desire," she purred. He rolled his eyes, annoyed by her transparent tactics and itching to knock teeth down her throat with a well-placed kick.

"I reckon you didn't come to town on horseback. If you had, patrols would have hailed you down and sent you away. That means you came through the well. So, my first question is—who's in charge, and what's their goal?"

The woman smiled, eyeing him like a piece of meat for a while before responding.

"Lucanos be his name—son of Satan, and Dragon of the Abyss. His mission is quite simple: to claim every soul on earth for hell."

"Who killed all the fucking horses and ruined every wagon in town?!" Roy barked from across the room, his eyes bloodshot.

"That would be his 'sheep'."

A knowing look settled across her face, lips curled into a smirk.

"Sheep? What the hell's that supposed to mean?" Clint demanded. The woman leaned forward, eyes boring holes into his.

"Since it's too late for you to stop it, I'll tell you. The little ones from your town's orphanage belong to darkness. With your people unable to escape, his grand design shall come to fruition. Oh, how I ache to see daemons raping you all for eternity."

"Oh, what a crock of shit! I'm going to check the orphanage myself! Y'all keep an eye on this stupid sow!" he shouted, standing from the chair in which he sat. He stormed out the door with his revolvers drawn. The wench laughed—a shrill sound bereft of genuine joy. Walks glared in her direction, the mirth she displayed a direct affront to all the suffering inflicted around her.

"Shut your fucking mouth," he said, his knuckles white from the grip he held on the table. Louder brays met his words in response, his rage stoking into an all-consuming fire. Tears rolled down the harlot's porcelain skin, her mockery intensifying to the point of hysterical fits.

"I said—SHUT THE FUCK UP!" he screamed, shooting to his feet. The most-empty bottle atop the table fell to the floor and shattered. He strode to the door of her cell, kicking the chair before it aside. He cut his eyes meaningfully toward Roy. The sheriff hobbled over, clearly inebriated, his breath like a distillery. He produced a key from his breast pocket and slotted it into the keyhole. The iron door popped open with a rusty squeal, a barrier no longer between Walks and the woman who'd invoked his searing anger.

"Are you going to kill me, tribeless one?"

He sneered and shook his head. Confusion flitted across her face, an inquisitive look replacing the smirk there.

"No, seeing as you likely have a few souls inside you that'll get set loose and feed the well if I do. Roy, would you mind getting me a flat piece of metal nice and hot?"

The sheriff nodded, making his way to the back room. Walks removed the lantern from the table. He lifted the woman, tossing her roughly atop the table. Her careless facade crumbled as their eyes met.

"I'm not gonna kill you, but I doubt it'll be much better in the long run. Have I told you about my newfound love for stumpy whores?"

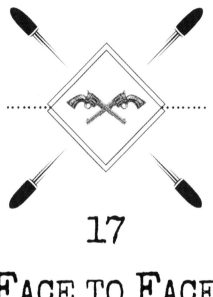

17

FACE TO FACE

U pon the return of his flock, Lucanos set his ultimate plan in motion. He ordered the children to line up, daubing each of their foreheads with a drop of his blood. It ensured their souls would cling to him instead of feeding the well. After this step, the dice could fall where they like. Even if his forces failed, no living soul would escape Murrayville so long as he drew breath.

Satan's son gazed upon the little ones, anticipation roaring up within. They stood quietly, blood splattered on their clothes, their hands. He drew his dagger, the cruel edge shining as it came free of its sheath. With no further ado, he clutched the first child by a handful of hair, wrenching the boy's head backward. He slit his throat in one mean cut, blood spurting as the boy fell to his knees, breath gurgling wetly as he twitched and died.

Lucanos stepped to the left and did the same to the next brat, then the next, until they all lay dying at his feet. Once they'd all perished, tiny motes of blue light rose from their corpses, revolving around him like planets to a sun. It was time.

He spoke aloud an incantation with words older than any language in existence, formless and infinitely deep. His voice rose and fell—tides of a dying sea set to drown the world in its own blood. His eyes glowed red, his form vibrating with the colossal power surging through him. Each syllable was a cracking whip, the air surging with a malevolent current. His spell ended, the last sound uttered still echoing from the walls. An explosion boomed overhead, summoning a grin to his face.

Clint sprinted with all his might, the whiskey from before sloshing around in his gut. He ignored the unpleasant sensation as best he could, the muscles in his legs ablaze. Years of drinking and smoking were finally catching up to him, and at the least opportune time. Bad luck or no luck, as usual.

Dust kicked up from his desperate strides, his breath short with exertion. He ran through the alley between Wrangler's Rest and a general store, turning right. So intent was he on his destination that he didn't notice the large rock underfoot. He sprawled on his belly with a pained grunt, vomit surging from his mouth and nostrils.

His sinuses burned, teeth coated in bitter and gritty bile. After spitting and taking a moment to steady himself, Clint rose to his feet. He set his hat back upon his head, grateful it hadn't fallen in the line of fire of his gastric purge. Just as he set to run again, a noise erupted from seemingly all directions. Blinding light nearly seared his eyes, red in hue and radiating great heat.

Clint gaped at the fiery dome now encasing all of Murrayville. If he couldn't put an end to this catastrophe, it might as well have been the lid for a coffin. He absent-mindedly pulled a smoke from the tin in his breast pocket, lit it, and resumed his run toward the orphanage. He knew it was too late, but his wrath heralded him onward into the fray.

The front door of the orphanage shattered on impact from his kick. He stepped in, his sense instantly assaulted by the rich iron and copper of blood. It was dark inside, his eyes reluctantly adjusting to the gloom. Small shapes took form in the hallway as he stepped forward. Grim laughter met his ears from deeper within the doomed dwelling.

"I don't know what you think is so goddamn funny, cocksucker, but I'm aimin' to wreck your mood!" Clint barked.

Louder peals of mirth rang out at his words. He took another step, the dim shapes on the floor now defined. Six children lay slaughtered and left to rot. Their throats had been slashed to ribbons, pale vertebrae peaking through, cooling blood caked a half-inch thick on the floor beneath them. Sightless eyes stared at the ceiling, blue lips half parted. Each stab of laughter brought his mind back to that dreadful night in Mexico. He screamed, stomping toward the mocking sound, his Colts raised and pulse hammering.

Clint wasn't prepared for his foe's appearance when he crossed the threshold into the kitchen. Although he had put little thought into what Lucanos might look like, the sight still unsettled him. Golden hair framed a fair face with a chiseled jawline, black silk making up the entirety of the arch daemon's garb. He'd have resembled a king of olden times, aside from the serpent's eyes cast in his direction. Those eyes challenged him, sharp teeth glistening in slobber from his murderous grin. With one glance, he knew those teeth were meant to devour flesh.

"Well? I'm waiting, gunslinger—wreck my mood," Lucanos jeered. Clint pulled the triggers on his Colts, and everything went sideways. Satan's son lunged to the right, both rounds smashing into the wall behind him. He moved toward him with a speed the bounty hunter had never seen before. A glint in the arch daemon's hand caught his eye, clearly a blade by his motions. He let out a quick breath, his eyes glowed, and time's cruel pendulum lulled.

Lucanos' expression was one of pure disbelief. Sadly, there was little time to cherish it. Each second of his ability felt more draining than it ever had before. There was no time to waste. He shot him in the chest with both barrels; the bullets crumpling like tin cans upon his hard flesh. A crack had formed in the hide where he'd shot, as well as singed holes in the dark prince's tunic. He cocked the hammers back and fired again. This time, black blood fountained from his attack.

Despite the temporal flux, his foe still moved, albeit slowly. His trajectory was not toward him, but toward escape through the hallway, he realized. Clint fired again, his shots glancing off of Lucanos' right shoulder. The flesh must have been softer there, because another gout of blood sprung loose where the bullets struck. Just as he lined up another shot, his grasp on time ceased. Lucanos' laughter was now screams of pain and rage, instead. The door slammed behind him as he fled. He panted, sinking to his knees on the kitchen floor.

An orb of golden light formed at the center of the room, a familiar voice beginning to speak. Clint looked up at it with weary eyes.

"Bearer of my blood, I bring news. By stepping foot into mankind's realm, Lucanos has breached a pact forged long ago between heaven and hell. Considering this transgression, our Lord has bid me to impart wisdom to you. There is a way to not only close the rift-gate, but vanquish Satan's son from existence forevermore."

JAMES FISHER

18

CUT DOWN TO SIZE

L ucanos sat in an empty barn with his back propped against a wall. Hot blood ran from his chest, over his shoulder. Things weren't supposed to go this way! He growled to himself, rage boiling his insides. The Whore had yet to return, and given his luck with the gunslinger, she was likely dead or captured. Every aspect of his plan had failed so far, but he refused to accept defeat so easily.

With so much of his blood readily available, his next course of action was clear. He focused on what little power he had left, extending his awareness beyond his body, combing through the souls of Murrayville for ideal candidates. He sought feeble minds, and within a few minutes of scrying, he'd found them. Two junkies and a retard—ripe for the picking. He said a small incantation aloud for each of them, then slumped back against the barn wall from the exertion. Everything came down to this.

Leroy Stetson rose from the dingy bed in which he and his wife lay, the taste of opium still caked upon his tongue. Susanne sat upright, her eyes bloodshot like his, both their hearts hammering rapidly. They stood, silently pulling on their boots as they trudged through the filthy confines of their small cabin to the world outside of it. It had been over a week since they'd gone out, and despite a subconscious questioning, they walked, unbidden, of their consent or thoughts.

Was this real, or some strange dream? After a decade of heavy opium use, it was hard to say anymore. The pair walked on, either oblivious or indifferent to the distant sounds of townsfolk gathering. A slowly dawning horror washed over him, each step carrying both him and his wife towards an irreversible doom. The Well of Torment called, and they were helpless to do anything other than obey.

Another damned soul came up on their right—the local mongoloid, Bertram. They walked as close to the well as they could. Nearly two hundred daemon corpses were piled around the structure in bloodied ruins. Flies swarmed about the midden heap of rotting flesh, maggots crawling from open wounds and ruptured eye sockets. They stepped over the bodies they could, then resorted to crawling atop them when that was no longer feasible.

Red flesh sloughed and ripped under their weight, blood and excrement oozing out as they inched closer toward the construct which would consume them. The stench made his mouth water; the flesh sinking into itself as he moved. Bertram reached the well first, his messy brown hair soaked in sweat. He smiled, then extended his hand toward it.

Leroy wanted to scream, to run as far away as he could. What he desired was no longer relevant, his eyes weeping as the simple one placed a pudgy hand upon the well. His mouth dropped agape, drool running down his stubbled chins. An inhumanly anguished scream ripped from his throat.

His cheeks sank inward, flesh melting into a pinkish goop that flowed down, revealing muscle tissue that gleamed beneath. His eyes sizzled, then ejaculated yellow jelly down his dissolving cheeks. He screamed until he ceased to be. His body was now a withered husk, still gripping the well with a fleshless hand.

Despite every fiber of Leroy's being begging him to stop, his hand extended towards the same fate Bertram faced. Susanne locked eyes with him, years of kinship shining through the power guiding and controlling them.

"I love you," he said.

"I love you, too."

They held one another's free hand, then touched the well. Their lips met—a kiss at the end of the world. Together, they melted, their last embrace eternal. Shortly after, green lightning shot up from the depths of the well.

"EVERY MAN, WOMAN, AND CHILD CAPABLE OF SHOOTING A GUN, LINE UP!" Roy shouted. He wobbled slightly on his feet, but it appeared to Clint that adrenaline had sobered him up some. Within ten minutes of giving the sheriff his plan(the part he needed to know, anyhow), nearly two hundred people had already gathered. Most of them still wore their bedclothes, but that didn't affect their ability to pull a trigger. An eager ferocity possessed them, a willingness to kill and die for their homes.

While Sheriff Gallagher inspected everyone's weapons, Irving Statler prepared the Gatling gun for yet another battle. He'd rolled out a crate of ammunition, and once the hopper was full, he dusted his palms off on his pant legs and sighed.

"I hope this is enough ammunition, because it's all I've got left," he said.

"If everything goes according to plan, we might not even need *that* much," Clint replied, secretly hoping his words were true. He placed a cigarette between his teeth, and as he lit it, lightning burst from the well. He squinted in the construct's direction, noting three desiccated human corpses that hadn't been there before. Lucanos had pulled yet another cheap trick, hoping to prevail. He spit, taking a long drag on his smoke as the roars of approaching dae-mons filled the hot air.

"Was that part of your plan?" Irving asked, going into a rumble of grim laughter. Clint nodded, pulling his Colts free of their holsters.

"Of course. Can't stop an invasion from hell with-out some daemons to kill, right?" The gunsmith laughed harder. Roy walked up to take his place at the Gatling, nodding at Clint.

Walks In Shadow came up, a leather leash in his hand. Looking at what lay at the other end sent Clint into a gale of laughter. The now-legless whore dragged behind, hands clawing at the collar around her neck. A perfectly shaped ass-groove trailed in her wake where she'd been dragged.

"That's quite a pet you got there, Walks."

"Thank you kindly. I figured I might as well make the end times fun while I still can."

Clint felt a pang of sadness looking upon his best friend. Things would be better this way. He'd just try to talk him out of it if he could. Only the gunslinger knew what it would *truly* take to set right the many wrongs inflicted upon Murrayville. He hoped his partner would under-stand when the time came.

Walks hitched the Whore to the Gatling, kicking her onto her belly. He sliced the dirt and blood-stained dress along its hem, leaving her ass and cunt out for the world to see.

"If the daemons decide to start raping, I'm volunteering you first to be bred," he hissed. He took his place alongside Clint and readied his bow.

Like so many moments in their life before, they found themselves in the calm before the storm. It was different this time, and he felt he couldn't afford to waste even a second. He turned to face his friend, their eyes locking.

"I've been thinkin' about our talk on the ride up here. You told me to stop pretending. Said I hadn't changed a bit. At the time, I figured you might be onto something. Now, I can safely say that you were dead wrong."

"We're a few minutes away from possibly dying, and you're trying to pick a fight?" Walks laughed.

"No, I just—when things get heavy, I need you to know that a man *can* change. Even men like us."

Before anything else could be said, daemons emerged from the well. Everything came down to these moments. Murrayville faced two fates: victory or death.

19

HELL LET LOOSE

Hell had sent some of their best this time. The daemons surging from the rift-gate were far larger and fiercer than the soldiers that preceded them. Muscles stood taut beneath red flesh, the army a blur of tooth and claw. Their roars rattled windows, their speed greater than their bulking forms suggested. Roy cranked the Gatling and shouted, "OPEN FIRE!"

Over two hundred firearms cracked, bullets flying in a torrential barrage of lead. Blood misted from wounded daemon flesh, hissing in the burning winds. Hellspawn caught rounds to the face, the chest, tumbling to the earth in a tangle of limbs. A few foes stumbled over their fallen allies, though most stomped their corpses flat underfoot, organs now a viscous paste baking on the hot sand.

Clint fired swift and true, his quarries collapsing lifelessly to the ground, black blood pooling beneath them. Walks In Shadow stood at his side, felling an equal number to his partner. Arrows impaled skulls, red eyes blinded, forevermore. The roar of battle enveloped all of Murrayville. Irving Stetler stood near Roy's right side, blasting the hellish army with a well-used pump-action twelve gauge. He shot again, missing wide, and as he fumbled to feed more shells into his shotgun, a daemon leapt at him, seizing him by the throat. It lifted him with a viciously clawed hand, his feet kicking helplessly a foot over the ground.

Walks shot the daemon through the eye, but too late. It tore the gunsmith's throat out, his carotid arteries spurting hot lifeblood in sanguine arcs. Both he and his killer fell down, wet gurgles hissing in the bald man's throat. Roy screamed, cranking the Gatling faster at the sight of his dead friend, rounds ripping Hellspawn asunder. Intestines and fluids coated the ground, the stench like sulfur.

They fought on, sparing nothing that moved. Another surge of lightning belched from the rift-gate. Despite this,

Clint felt the townsfolk' courage. It would take far worse to break their morale. The swarm had thinned significantly, shots slowing down as the combatants picked individual targets out from the pack.

War cries rang from every mouth, children included. Each slain foe seemed to whip them further into a blood-crazed frenzy. Their revelry halted to an abrupt sound—it drowned all other noise in the din. A deep roar echoed from the depths, bone-rattling and malevolent enough to chill the soul. Clint looked to Walks In Shadow, the pair nodding and bracing themselves for whatever came next.

Roy furrowed his brow, glaring at the people who'd faltered in their attack with great annoyance.

"DID I TELL YOU SONS OF BITCHES TO STOP?! PULL THOSE TRIGGERS UNTIL YOUR FUCKING FINGERS BREAK, THEN KEEP PULLING THEM FOR GOOD MEASURE!" he shouted.

Gunfire promptly resumed its breakneck pace—dense, white clouds of gun smoke filling the air with its heady bouquet. Thirty daemons dwindled to five, then none. The growling from the well shattered any pretense that victory had been achieved. Its volume swelled with each passing second. Clint felt the hairs on the back of his neck stand on end, the tension so thick he could hardly breathe.

He pulled a cigarette from the tin in his breast pocket, marveling that it was the last one. Fitting.

An arm the size of a man jutted through the portal, then another, a hulking brute rising from the portal. The Fellbaest stepped out of the well, his body easily nine feet tall. It was a colossal foe, nude and resembling an ogre from children's fairy tales, though the two-foot cock swinging between its knees would likely be omitted. As Clint reloaded his Colts, Walks In Shadow unhitched the Whore of Babylon, dragging her forwards as he shouted for Roy to cease fire.

The sheriff eyed him like he'd gone mad. Clint briefly held the same belief.

"Just trust me. I think this stinking ax-wound can be useful for something," Walks said with a grin. Roy rolled his eyes, then raised a clenched fist for a ceasefire. He dragged her a few more feet, then kicked her side, so that she rolled toward the Fellbaest.

It stopped its furious strides towards them, idly scratching its massive belly while eyeing the offering presented to him. Then, a lurid expression crossed its hideous face, and it lifted her by the waist with one hand while the other fastidiously stroked its discolored and pus-oozing dick. The townsfolk went deathly silent, unable to look away as it lowered her over its ghastly member. Her pink lips splayed

127

upon its glans, blood pouring at the top of her cleft where he'd already ripped her.

Walks nudged Clint in the ribs, snapping him from his awestruck stupor.

"We gonna tag team this big bastard while he's distracted, or what? It won't take long for him to fuck that bitch in half." Clint nodded his acquiescence, and his partner disappeared. He stepped forth, Colts half-raised, as he endeavored to maintain a placid expression.

The Whore of Babylon screamed, her cunt soaking the Fellbaest's shaft in a creamy, bloody discharge. He worked her like a puppet, masturbating himself with her ruined hole, every inch of its phallus stuffed into her warm insides. It slowly looked up at Clint's approach, massive brows knitting downward, eyes constricting to dark slits.

"Easy there, big fella. I ain't gonna take your tasty treat from you. Unlike us, it looks like you can have a taste without losing your soul. You know, I'm almost jealous!"

He took another tentative step toward the daemon, which growled a louder warning in response.

"Fuck you, too, then, you ugly motherfucker."

Clint fired a round with each pistol, the Fellbaest's eyes exploding in a fountain of blood and shredded ocular tissue.

It dropped the barely breathing whore to the ground, screaming and grasping futilely at its ruined globes. Black blood poured from the gory chasms, and as the Fellbaest rushed toward him, his eyes glowed. Time froze, the daemon suspended mid-stride with its arms outreached to crush his skull.

He patiently re-loaded from the two shots, watching as blood poured from its right ear. Walks appeared atop the brute, his knife slipping in and out of its brain until it flowed in a slimy river. He jumped down from the daemon, wiping his blade clean as he took his place alongside Clint.

"When Lucanos shows, coat that blade with some of your own blood and sucker him. I can only slow time if he's too close to me," Clint whispered.

Time resumed, the Fellbaest collapsing lifeless to the ground. Silence seemed to stretch for an eternity—then the townsfolk began to cheer. Walks ignored their premature celebration, leaning in to his partner so others wouldn't hear.

"Won't stabbing him in general do the trick?"

"Just trust me. There's power in the blood."

"Fine. I'll do my part. I just hope this wor—"

A woman's shriek interrupted their exchange. Clint turned, pistols raised, while he scanned for the cause of the commotion. One cry soon became many, panic spreading among the people like wildfire. Guns fired, mass confusion ramping up with unrelenting speed.

"It's Lucanos. Has to be," Clint hissed.

"I'm cloaking. Slow him down as much as you can."

Walks In Shadow drew his knife and sliced his palm, coating the blade with blood. The Loathsome Two gave one another a nod, then he vanished.

Clint braced himself, knowing their foe had already slain a score of innocent lives. He drew deeply from his inner well of strength, the fate of mankind hinging upon this moment. For the last time, his eyes glowed a blinding, golden burst—and time's cruel pendulum lulled.

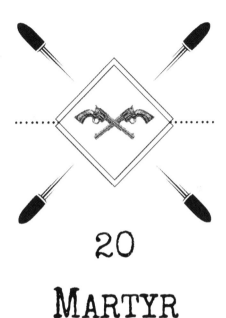

20

MARTYR

Walks In Shadow could feel Lucanos amid the chaos, like a ray of nauseating cold. A blond woman lay at the feet of the surging flock of people. Her throat had been ripped free, pale bits of her spinal cord shining through ruined flesh. Where there was one corpse, there was sure to be more. He slipped through the teeming mass, eyes always hunting his mark.

Another scream rang out over the din. He moved toward it, the vivid red of fresh blood glinting in the hot air. There he was—the source of everyone's woes, a gleeful grin upon his cruelly regal face. People scattered wherever he stood, though his speed denied any hope of escape. He stabbed a young boy between the eyes, blurring away as gunshots struck where he'd just stood.

Time halted around them, the surrounding chaos like a still-life painting from a psychopath's dream journal. He stepped through the motionless people, his eyes never losing sight of his foe. Lucanos still moved, albeit slowly. If Walks wanted to end this, perfect timing was imperative. He drew closer, looking for a weakness he could exploit to his advantage. There it was—a large wound between his pectorals, likely a parting gift from Clint.

Despite the temporal rift, Lucanos showed no signs of relenting in his bloodbath. He leapt from side to side, bullets never so much as grazing his clothes. He placed his cruel hands around a middle-aged woman's neck, ripping upwards as she screamed and her eyes bulged near to bursting. Her skull came free, the spinal cord still attached. It dangled like a grisly kite-string, fluids pooling beneath it before he carelessly tossed it over his shoulder.

Walks knew he could wait no longer to strike. For the first time in his life, fear held his gut in an icy grip. He didn't fear for his life, but the lives of the townspeople surrounding him. Everything was at stake.

Lucanos swiveled, his eyes falling upon a young girl. His intent was clear, his teeth dripping slobber and dagger raised high. If Walks didn't make his move now, there might not be another chance. The arch daemon launched towards his prey.

Lucanos' expression shifted from gleeful bloodlust to incomprehensible anguish. He looked at the wound on his chest, bright light flaring and flesh loudly sizzling. Walks released his cloak, finally face-to-face with his foe. His knife sat hilt deep in his chest, fist clenched on its handle in a deathgrip.

Something dawned on him. Despite their proximity, the arch daemon made no efforts to retaliate over the blade in his chest. In fact, he was as motionless as everyone else. Clint's words came flashing back to him: "There's power in the blood." He laughed, spitting in Lucanos' face.

"All that dark magick and conniving—foiled by the *fucking* Loathsome Two. Does that sting? I hope it does."

Walks savored the indignant glower he received for a moment, then looked towards the well. Souls drifted toward it, siphoned by its insatiable hunger. What concerned him more was the sight of Clint walking toward the dark construct.

"WHAT THE HELL ARE YOU DOING?!" he shouted. His partner only smiled in his direction and continued walking.

There's power in the blood.

Understanding filled Walks In Shadow, the truth like icy needles in his spine. Ever since speaking to Gabriel, Clint had been acting a little odd. It all made sense now.

A man can change. Even men like us.

He screamed a wordless plea to his partner. Clint smiled, tipped his hat, and threw himself into the Well of Torment.

The well groaned, white rays bursting from its depths. Those radiant beams soon overpowered its dreadful green glow. The earth quaked underfoot, the black construct rattling. Its cruel barbs fell to the ground and crumbled to dust. Radiant fissures formed at its base, spreading and converging into an intricate spider web.

All stood in deafening silence. Every eye rested upon the rift-gate, the seconds like hours. The well shuddered, then settled, then shuddered again—and exploded with a tooth-rattling boom. Dust plumed out in a vast circle from where it had stood, the air now coarse and biting. His trance was interrupted by Lucanos' moans of pain.

He fixed his mouth to further taunt the arch daemon, then stopped when he saw Clint's plan coming to fruition. He stood, paralyzed by the blooded blade, his body twitching in place. His form seemed to undulate—expanding and contracting in ways that made the stomach churn. Walks snatched his knife free and stepped back just in time. Like a dying star, Lucanos' imploded into nothingness, and everything went blindingly white.

When his sight returned, it was as if he'd been transported to another place entirely. No fiery dome sat overhead now, only blue sky. The sun was no longer a serpent's eye, but simply a star millions of miles away. He slumped to his knees, and whether for joy or grief, he wept.

The mounds of daemon corpses withered to ash, scattering in the breeze sweeping in. Only the human dead remained, many being mourned over actively. Roy sat hunched on all fours behind the Gatling gun, spewing vomit and promising himself he'd never drink again. Despite all the pain, Walks could only laugh as tears streamed his face.

Gusts of cool wind came upon Murrayville, heavy clouds shifting back into their rightful place. Then, for the first time in months, it began to rain. It started with small, timid droplets, but soon came down in sheets. He could practically hear the earth sigh in relief as the water met it, steam rising from the hissing dirt.

Those not mourning their dead stood in the downpour with extended arms and upturned faces. After so much turmoil and anguish, the beauty of it all was overwhelming. He sat in the rain, the last fifteen years playing in his mind. Though he had his flaws, Clint was about the best friend a man could ask for. He would be missed.

Once his grief subsided, he stood and surveyed the aftermath of the battle. Roy lay on his belly, still grumbling to himself and fighting waves of nausea. He smiled and offered him a hand up. The sheriff accepted his help, swaying on his feet once he fully stood. After attempting to let the old-timer walk unaided and watching him fall seven times, he couldn't contain his mirth.

"Come on, Roy. I'll get you to the station," he said with a grin, throwing the drunk's arm over his shoulder and leading him. They stepped slowly through the spots where the dead lay, stepping into the station as the rain continued to beat down. The smell of blood still hung in the still air. It would fade with time, like many other things.

Sheriff Gallagher made a drunken beeline toward his chair, his weight plopping down on it gracelessly. Walks fixed himself a nip of gin, and by the time he turned around, the old man was already snoring. Sleep didn't sound like such a bad idea. He made himself comfortable on a cot in an empty cell and drifted off.

Upon waking, he found himself in the company of a much more sober Roy. They had a cup of coffee and sat in silence between sips. The gravity of everything they'd endured was just beginning to show. What words could make right the loss of a dear friend? Once the sheriff finished his cup, he toyed with his mustache for a moment and cleared his throat.

"Walks, I think our buddy Clint knew things might end this way. The night y'all rode in, he told me that his pay was to go to you, should anything go awry. He might've looked like a chewed-up cow patty, but the son of a bitch was smarter than he let on. So—that'll put one hundred thousand dollars in your pocket for your troubles."

Walks nearly choked on his sip of coffee. The figure he'd just floated like it was nothing—more money than he'd ever made bounty hunting. Enough to settle down. Roy laughed good-naturedly and patted him on the shoulder.

"What are you aimin' to do with all that money? Gonna buy a whorehouse for personal use?" he asked, going into chuckles.

Walks smiled and shook his head. He went to the liquor cabinet and fixed them each a shot of whiskey. Roy's eyes bulged, and he attempted to wave away the drink, taking it after a sharp glance. They held their glasses aloft, and he said the only toast that made sense.

"To Clint."

EPILOGUE

I t was a pleasant morning in springtime. The birds sang, and lush green lay wherever the eye could see. The sweet aroma of honeysuckle floated in the morning air. Walks In Shadow took all the beauty in as he watered his garden.

Golden rays of sunlight glimmered off of dew-laden grass, butterflies flitting aimlessly in the flowery meadows in the distance. In the decade since Clint died, he'd grown accustomed to savoring the little things more. The hurt had healed from a bleeding wound to pink scar tissue—memories that might have once drawn tears now only brought fond feelings.

Life was funny in that way. Death's color seemed not so harsh as he grew older. All good came with bad. He'd endure all his worst days with his best friend before not experiencing them at all. He sighed and brought his watering can to the tool shed along the east side of his cabin. After hanging it from a hook, he walked onto the front porch and sat in his oak-wood rocking chair.

"Is that you on the porch, Walks?" Molly called from the living room. Even after a decade of marriage, the sound of her voice still drove him wild.

"Yeah, baby, it's me."

A moment later, the screen door rasped open behind him. Molly walked in front of him, poking her lips out for a kiss. As he leaned in, she pulled him tight by a fistful of hair, her tongue swimming with his before letting him go.

"Hey, big guy."

"Hey yourself, good looking. Chorin's done for the day. Is there anything you've a mind to do?"

"I think a picnic in the meadow would be wonderful. The children will love it!" she said, bouncing on her tip-toes and twirling a red curl with her finger excitedly.

"A picnic, it is! Get the children ready. I've got to go pay my respects."

Molly nodded, a sad understanding etched on her fine features. Walks stood up and hiked toward the south side of his property. He stopped amid a dense grove of pines where he'd built a cross.

"You've been gone ten years. Seems like just yesterday we were bickering over whether to rob or kill that stagecoach driver. I miss you every day, even if you talked too much," he said with a smile.

"Molly and I are taking the kids on a picnic soon. I just wanted to say hello. And—thank you, Clint. Thank you."

With that, he turned and headed back towards his cabin.

A man can change.

For a decade, those words had echoed in his mind. He'd used them to guide his life, and now had a wife, children, and McCoy Farm, which was beginning to yield profit. He took a last glance at his friend's grave, then walked into the sunlight. His family was waiting for him.

ABOUT THE AUTHOR

James Fisher is an Extreme Horror/Splatterpunk author from Central Louisiana. When he's not wrestling his daughters or emitting flatulence on his wonderful wife, James is plinking away at a book on his trusty Smith-Corona typewriter, Kurt. James is a disabled veteran of the United States Army, metalhead, and an enthusiast for all things gore, bizarre, and depraved.

ALSO BY JAMES FISHER

Spiritcrusher's Crusade
Spiritcrusher's Crusade II: Flesh Cabal
Bussin' Down
Also Featured in:
Written In Carnage

Made in the USA
Columbia, SC
11 December 2024

47733051R00090